GROWN *ass* WOMAN

a Novel by

EARTHA GATLIN

AHTRAE PUBLISHING, LLC

www.therealearthagatlin.com

Published in the United States by Ahtrae Publishing, LLC
Dallas, Texas 2025

www.therealearthagatlin.com

Cover design by Cheakina.

Editor Chandra Sparks Splond

Book formatting by Sienna Arts

ISBN: 979-8-218-63001-0

Library of Congress Cataloging in Publication Data

Name: Gatlin, Eartha, author

Description: Dallas, Texas: Ahtrae Publishing, LLC, 2025

Identifiers: Library of Congress Control Number (LCCN): 2025904312

10 9 8 7 6 5 4 3 2 1

Printed in the United States of America

Also, by Eartha Gatlin

The Chronicles of Bria Twon
Hey You, What About Me, Bria Twon?
Who Told You Family Was Perfect, Bria Twon?

*This book is dedicated to all my grown ass ladies, I see you.
Especially my sister, Lawanda and friend Veronica*

Acknowledgements

To my Heavenly Father, the author and finisher of my faith — thank You, again and again. I could have never imagined being here, holding book number four in my hands. How cool is that?

I'm deeply grateful for the courage You've given me to create something for myself while adding something, however small, to the literary world. I know I'm not "renowned" just yet, but I am genuinely happy with how my steps have been ordered and with the progress each new day brings.

Thank you to my readers and supporters — the ones who follow, encourage, and pick up my books. I write to entertain, but also to share relatable stories about women of my tribe and era — stories we don't always hear but absolutely need to. My goal isn't to demean anyone, male or female, of any persuasion. Instead, I aim to empower women and offer glimpses into perspectives and lifestyles that might not mirror your own.

Does that mean I'm saying you should try any of these things? Absolutely not. What I am saying is this: consider, observe, laugh a little, and keep an open mind. It's all about reading, learning, and evolving — and there's no one "right" way to do that.

Thank you for sharing this journey with me. I hope you find my work authentic enough to pass along, and I look forward to meeting you again in the pages of my next book. Until then — enjoy!

With gratitude,
Eartha

Quotes

"The course of true love never did run smooth."
A Midsummer Night's Dream (Act 1, Scene 1)
Shakespeare

"Far too many games that people play..."
Maze featuring Frankie Beverly

Contents

GROWN *ass* WOMAN

a Novel by

EARTHA GATLIN

Chapter 1

Joanie: Unfinished Portraits

Sometimes I simply cannot believe the things people say and do—men, specifically. Why do some men find it so damn hard to commit or just be honest? Back in the day, I could understand it better because we were all young, sowing our wild oats, caught up in the fun and games. But now? At the grown-ass age of sixty-four? I have a very low tolerance for bullshit.

Let me explain: Me, Joanie Townsend. Twice divorced. Mother to two beautiful grown daughters. Owner of a successful art gallery. Witty, slightly cynical, yet somehow still hopeful. I've seen it all, and while I'm not delusional, I still like to believe that love—real, committed, honest love—is possible. Call me old school, but I still live by the scripture, Proverbs, 18:22, Whoso findeth a wife findeth a good thing... I don't want to be out here chasing a man, searching high and low. I am the good thing—or at least, I'd like to believe I am.

Steam curled in the air as I ran a towel over my damp skin, fresh from the shower. My mornings were usually peaceful—coffee brewing, soft jazz humming from the Apple HomePod, my mind already shifting to the work waiting for me at the gallery. But today, that peace had been hijacked.

The face of Tremaine Adkins, one of my besties, filled my phone screen, her expression a mix of disbelief and irritation.

"I am completely baffled by the audacity of some men," she declared, shaking her head. "Why in the hell are you even dealing with this shit, Joanie?"

I sighed, propping the phone into the mount on my bathroom mirror as I massaged moisturizer into my face. Tremaine goes on speaking without giving me a chance to respond.

"Girl, what did you say that muthafucka said again?" Her voice rang through the speakers—sharp, no-nonsense, as familiar to me as my own reflection.

I took a deep breath. "He said he'd have to find another window to come see me again."

"And just what the hell does that mean?" Her voice rose, laced with irritation.

"Your guess is as good as mine."

Tremaine didn't hesitate. "I'll tell you what it means—your ass will get in where you fit in. Sounds to me like he's not making you a priority at all. Didn't you say it's been months since you last saw that nigga?"

I sighed, rolling my eyes even though I knew she was right. "Yeah. It's been a few months, but—"

"No *buts*. You're worth more than sporadic meetups. What's keeping you tethered to that man? I don't know when you're gonna hit rock bottom with him, but damn, Joanie, he's a narcissistic jerk. You sit around waiting for crumbs of his time—for what? Forty-five minutes of attention?"

I hesitated, already bracing for her reaction before I calmly responded to her question. "It was after he'd left. He called while driving back to his hotel, said we'd do dinner, then a couple of hours later, I got a text. Said he wasn't feeling well. No. Wait. He said he was tired, had an early flight, and that he'd find another window to come again. Then we could do dinner and maybe I could show him around Dallas."

The second I said it out loud, I cringed. Hearing the words made them sound even more absurd.

"*Hmph.*" Tremaine sucked her teeth. "Honey, you wanna know what I would've told that bastard?"

Of course she didn't wait for me to answer.

"I would've said, 'Nah, bruh. You keep that window. Matter of fact, that mutha is shut. You can keep your tired ass right where you're at.' What the fuck did he even bother coming for? 'Cause it damn sure wasn't to see *you*, Joanie. He must've had other business in Dallas 'cause that shit ain't adding up."

Everything she said, I had already thought about. Over and over, I'd replayed the entire situation before I even told her.

One thing about me, I never felt like a needy chick. I didn't check up on a man, didn't go snooping through his phone. If anything, I gave him too much rope, believing we were too grown for games. But this? *This* was a whole new level of bullshit.

I was done.

Or at least, I thought I was.

Tremaine was in full bestie big sister mode now and on a roll, and there was no stopping her.

"He doesn't take you to dinner. He doesn't treat you like you're special. Hell, he barely treats you like you exist. So, what is it? Is the dick that good?"

I sighed, still unclothed, I walked through the comfort of my home, glancing around my living room, seeking solace in the familiar pieces hanging on the walls—art I'd collected over the years that felt more like old friends than decoration. A small smile crept across my lips. Leave it to Tremaine to hit me with the raw truth, no chaser. "You don't have to put it like that."

"Well, somebody's got to. You're my girl, Joanie. I hate seeing you let this man play in your face like this. You deserve better."

I knew Tremaine wasn't trying to hurt me, but her words cut deep because they were true. Jackson *was* playing me, and I was letting him. There was no other way to spin it. Yet even as Tremaine ripped the situation apart with her usual brutal honesty, I still clung to a sliver of something—hope, maybe? Stupidity? Who the hell knows?

Tremaine's voice softened. "Joanie, you're sixty-four years old. A beautiful, accomplished woman with a business, a home, and a good heart. You shouldn't be begging for a man to treat you right. That nigga should be begging for *you*. Period."

She was right. Of course, she was right. But why was it so hard for me to let Jackson go? Maybe it was because I'd been hopeful for so long. Hopeful that one day he'd wake up and see the woman standing in front of him. A woman who deserved more than breadcrumbs.

But deep down, I knew better. And maybe tonight, just maybe, I'd start acting like I knew better. Then, the realization came out of the blue, and something in me finally clicked. I couldn't ignore the nagging feeling any longer. So I trusted my gut, pulled out my phone, and started doing a little research of my own. It didn't take long to find what I had always suspected—confirmation staring back at me in plain sight.

The soft hum of jazz floated through the gallery as I adjusted a painting on the far wall, my mind still lingering on my conversation with Tremaine from yesterday. Over coffee this morning, we'd confirmed our lunch plans, both agreeing there was more to unpack about *him*—though I wasn't sure I had the energy to keep rehashing the same dead-end situation.

I sighed, smoothing my hands down my smock, forcing my thoughts back to work. But just as I reached for my tablet, the chime of the gallery door pulled me from my daze.

I sat up straighter, glancing toward the entrance.

Maxwell Carter—Max to those who knew him well—strode inside with the effortless confidence that always preceded him.

Tall, channeling that debonair-looking Idris Elba persona, giving him a perfect balance of distinguished and mischievous, he had the kind of presence that made people take notice.

I had always admired the way he carried himself—assured, but never arrogant. But today...something about him felt different. The usual easy grin was absent, replaced by an expression I couldn't quite read.

"Joanie," he greeted, his voice smooth as ever, but there was a weight behind it.

"Max." I smiled, setting my tablet down. "Back so soon? What brings you in today?"

He hesitated for half a second before stepping closer, hands casually tucked into the pockets of his tailored slacks. "Needed one more piece for the condo."

I arched a brow. "*Needed,* or just an excuse to stop by and say hello?"

That familiar grin flickered back for a moment before he exhaled, shaking his head. "Can't a man appreciate good art and good company at the same time?"

I smirked. "If that's your way of saying you can't resist the art in my gallery, I'll allow it."

He chuckled, but his gaze lingered a second too long, like he was deciding whether or not to say something else.

I tilted my head, studying him. "You okay, Max?"

For a moment, he said nothing. Then, with a slow nod, he glanced around the gallery. "Yeah. Just...thinking."

I knew better than to press, but something told me Max Carter hadn't just come for art today.

I gestured toward the new collection near the back. "Come on. Let's find something that speaks to you."

And maybe, just maybe, I'd figure out what was really on his mind.

"Max," I said warmly, turning to face him as we neared the back, "so what really brings you in today? Did you forget a spot? That was quite a large purchase you made last week; I didn't expect to see you back so soon. I mean, not that I don't value your business."

He flashed that same magnetic smile—the one that had women of all ages tripping over themselves. "Joanie, no, no. Everything here is perfect, as always. I was just thinking about something you said when I was here last week, although you know how much I'm drawn to your art—hell, if I could, I'd buy every damn piece in this place."

I shot him a knowing look. "Cut the crap, Max. We both know you can. So, level with me: What's really on your mind?"

His smile faltered just slightly, his hands slipping out of his pockets, clasping together as if pleading for a favor. "Well, I was wondering if I could impose on you for something. It's...somewhat of a personal matter."

That caught me off guard. I had no idea what Max could possibly need from me outside of art. And the sudden shift in his energy made me instinctively put some space between us.

I busied myself with adjusting a canvas on the cutting table, trying to shake the unease creeping in. "Sure," I said carefully. "As long as it's not about my art."

"What man in his right mind doesn't appreciate your fine art?" Max said smoothly, his signature charm in full effect. Then, leaning in slightly, he lowered his voice like he was about to share a secret. "But let me cut to the chase, Joanie. I need some advice."

I arched a brow, amused. "Advice? From me?" I teased. "Now I *know* you're up to something."

He scratched the back of his bald head, a rare tell I'd seen only a handful of times. Max Carter didn't get uncomfortable—yet, here he was, shifting under my gaze.

Max chuckled, but there was a flicker of unease in his usually confident demeanor. "You're the wisest woman I know, Joanie. Given our history—and all the art deals we've navigated together—I figured you'd understand my situation better than most."

I arched a brow, folding my arms. "Max, let's be clear. Our 'history' is strictly business, unless you count all those times you've used our meetings to pick my brain about women."

He smirked, caught. "Exactly. That's the kind of history I mean."

I couldn't deny it. At this moment Max had my undivided attention. "Go on," I said, settling in. "Should I pour me a drink?"

And if he scratched the back of his bald head one more time, I was going to scream. Max had all the behaviors I'd come to recognize in someone either caught in a lie or on the verge of revealing a secret they'd been carrying too long and didn't know how to confess. The Max Carter I was used to didn't get uncomfortable, yet here he was, right in front of me, rubbing the back of his neck to his head, back to his neck, fidgeting from foot to foot, all under the weight of whatever was coming next, all while I'm doing my best not to scream, *Bruh, calm down!*

"It's about the women in my life."

I tilted my head. "*Women?* Plural?"

He let out a slow breath and nodded. "Yeah. Plural."

I didn't bother hiding my skepticism. "And let me guess: They're starting to expect more from you?"

He exhaled again, this time deeper, his gaze drifting toward the artwork on the walls as if searching for the right words. "I care about all of them. Deeply. But they're starting to ask for things I'm not sure I can give—commitment, exclusivity." He rubbed a hand over his beard. "I never claimed to be a one-woman man, Joanie, but lately...I'm starting to think I'm the problem."

His words hung in the air. It wasn't every day that a man admitted he might be the issue. And yet, the more he spoke, the more something about his tone unsettled me.

"Max," I said carefully, "let me get this clear. Again, soooo, you're seeing more than one woman? Two? Three?"

He didn't answer immediately. Instead, his gaze drifted toward a painting on the wall—a chaotic swirl of reds and blacks. Finally, he nodded. "Three. And they all think they're the only one."

I stared at him, my stomach twisting slightly. I didn't know whether to laugh, curse him out, or pour us both a drink.

Max let out a deep sigh, his gaze locking onto mine with a rare seriousness. "Real talk, not only are you the wisest woman I know, Joanie—and I don't just mean in business—but I've watched you over the years. I adore how you carry yourself. Yeah, we've done plenty of art deals together, but it's more than that. I've always admired the way you see things. You don't judge, you just *get* people. I figured if anyone could help me make sense of this mess, it's you."

I remained in posture with folded arms, leaning back against the cutting table. I felt my irritation brewing. "Okay, Max, enough of the flattery. Let's cut to the chase—straight and no chaser. I mean, I'm no shrink, but damn, I have to ask. What happened to you as a child, man, seriously?"

He hesitated, rubbing a hand over his beard before finally exhaling. "I've always seen multiple women at a time, and now, it's starting to catch up with me. They're all amazing in their own way, but I can't commit to just one. Honestly, my career and being successful have always been my priority. Hell, maybe it does have something to do with my childhood. Who the hell knows?"

I stared at him for a beat before letting out a dry chuckle. "Max, how old are you now?"

He looked slightly taken aback but answered anyway. "Sixty-five."

I shook my head, amusement and exasperation mixing in equal measure. "Sixty-five, and still playing with fire—juggling multiple women like you're twenty-five?"

He exhaled, tapping his fingers on my counter. "I know, Joanie. It's risky, and I'm starting to feel the heat. That's why I came to you. I need to figure out what to do before everything blows up in my face."

I studied him for a moment before leaning forward, my tone softening. "Max, it's time to be honest—with them and with yourself. You're not some twenty-something year old out here wild and free. At this stage in life, playing games will only lead to one thing: disaster."

He nodded slowly, letting my words sink in. "You're right," he admitted. "I need to make some changes."

I placed a reassuring hand on his arm. "It's never too late to do the right thing, Max. Here's my take: All of what you're doing is cool if all the parties involved are consenting and are aware of their roles in the dynamics of the relationship. Your issue is that you, Max Carter, are misleading, deceiving the other parties involved and that, my friend, is a problem. Come clean, sir."

He let out a long breath, the weight of the conversation settling between us. And for the first time in a long time, Max Carter looked like a man who wasn't entirely sure of his next move.

But before Max could respond, the gallery door chimed again. I turned toward the entrance and froze. And to my surprise, Tremaine stood there, sunglasses perched on her head, looking back and forth between Max and me. Her smile faltered when her eyes landed on him.

"Max?" she said, her voice cautious.

Max's face went pale, but he managed a weak smile. "Hey, Tremaine."

Tremaine looked at me, then back at Max. "Joanie, what's he doing here?"

I blinked, realization dawning like a gut punch. I knew Tremaine knew Max, but something in her tone and disposition was different...off. I sensed something uncomfortable between them.

Max cleared his throat, visibly awkward now. "*Uh,* I should probably go."

Tremaine's gaze shot daggers at him. "Oh, you don't need to leave on my account." She turned to me. "Joanie, we need to talk."

The gallery felt suffocating after Tremaine's words. I watched Max shuffle awkwardly, and Tremaine's icy glare made it clear that leaving would likely be his best option for now.

"Tremaine, what's going on?" I asked, my voice tinged with confusion and frustration.

She turned to me, her expression softening slightly but still guarded. "Joanie, trust me, we need to talk. Privately."

Max took a hesitant step back, his hands raised in mock surrender. "I'll, *uh,* give you two some space."

"Don't trip on your way out," Tremaine muttered, never breaking eye contact with me.

Max slinked toward the exit, and the chime of the door echoed in the silence he left behind.

"Tremaine, what the hell was that? Are you trying to ruin my business? You can't just come in here disrespecting my clients like that. What's gotten into you?" I asked, crossing my arms.

She sighed, removing her sunglasses and tucking them into her purse. "Joanie, I've been meaning to tell you something about Max, but when we spoke earlier, I couldn't find the right words. And then I got this...feeling, like I needed to come here and say this to your face."

"A feeling?" I said, arching a brow.

"Yes, a feeling. And now I know why," she said, glancing toward the door where Max had just exited. "I didn't expect to walk in on that. I had no idea he'd be here."

I studied her, trying to piece together what she wasn't saying. "Just how well do you know Max, Tremaine?"

She hesitated, her fingers tightening on her purse strap. "I would say pretty damn well, Joanie."

Her words hit like a freight train, leaving me momentarily speechless. I blinked, shaking my head as if that would clear the disbelief. "You're kidding. You mean—"

"I wish I was," she replied, her voice steady but tinged with regret. "And before you ask, yes, I know he's seeing others. I didn't sign up for something serious, Joanie, but knowing he's a friend of yours and happens to be one of your best clients complicates things even more."

I stood there, my mind struggling to process Tremaine's revelation. Max, a long-time client and friend, had somehow entangled himself with one of my closest friends without my knowledge. The room seemed to tilt slightly, and I felt a cold sensation in the pit of my stomach. How had I been so oblivious? And now, to discover this connection in such a jarring manner. It was almost too much to fathom. Tremaine placed a hand on my arm.

"Joanie, instead of lunch, we need to talk in detail, but not here, and I don't think lunch will suffice. Come by my place tonight. I don't want to keep anything from you. We're friends—besties. You deserve the truth."

Still reeling, I nodded. "Alright. Tonight."

Chapter 2

Joanie: Confrontation Between Friends

I don't know how I got through the rest of that day. My head spun with questions, anger simmering just beneath the surface. When the gallery finally closed, I threw on my coat, grabbed my bag, and headed straight for Tremaine's house.

I bobbed and weaved through the Dallas traffic going north on Interstate 635 North. I rehearsed the words I wanted to say. By the time I arrived at her driveway, the edge of my frustration had dulled into uncertainty. But one thing was clear: I needed answers.

When I stepped into Tremaine's home, the first thing I noticed was the chaos. Papers and books were scattered across the coffee table, a half-empty wineglass sat precariously on the arm of the sofa, and a stack of magazines teetered near the wall. Her workspace—what had probably been an organized corner at some point—was a haphazard mess of open folders, pens, and sticky notes plastered with scribbled reminders. It was a stark contrast to the composed, confident Tremaine I had come to know.

"Tremaine, you ever heard of decluttering?" I teased as I set my bag down on the one clear spot on her couch.

She laughed from the kitchen, her voice carrying over the sound of the kettle whistling. "You're lucky you caught me on a good day. I cleaned up last week."

I smirked but couldn't help noticing how the disarray mirrored the turmoil I sensed she was hiding. A part of me wanted to ask if everything was alright, but I had come here with my own storm to weather.

Moments later, Tremaine appeared with two mugs of lavender tea. She handed me one and settled into the oversized cushion chair across from me, her silver locs cascading over her shoulders. She crossed her legs as though she had all the time in the world.

"You've been quiet, Joanie," she said, studying me with that sharp, knowing gaze of hers. "So, let's hear it. What's on your mind? Say what you wanna say."

I set the cup down carefully, avoiding her eyes. "Tremaine, how long have you been seeing Max?"

She tilted her head slightly, almost amused. "Long enough to know better, if that's what you're asking."

"And so, like you do, I'm going to give it to you straight and no chaser. You told me you know about the others." My voice came out sharper than I intended.

Her expression didn't waver. "Of course I know, Joanie. I'm seventy years old, not seventeen. I didn't sign up for forever with that man. I'm enjoying him for what he is—no more, no less."

Her calm almost nonchalant tone threw me off. "But Tremaine...why? Why put yourself in that position?"

She laughed softly, shaking her head. "You think I'm being played. I'm not. I know exactly what I want, Joanie. And trust me, Max isn't the only man keeping me entertained."

I narrowed my eyes. "What does that mean?" Her lips curved into a slow, unapologetic grin. "There's someone else. His name's Malik. He's forty-three—yes, I know, twenty-seven years younger. And before you give me that look, don't. He's not some boy toy. The man is brilliant—a mechanical engineer with his own fleet of shops in various parts of the metroplex. He makes me laugh, listens better than most men twice his age, and Joanie, he looks at me like I'm the center of the damn universe."

I blinked, letting it sink in. "So Max is what, your Tuesday, and Malik is your Thursday?" She shrugged, unapologetic. "Something like that. Max is familiar—predictable in all the ways that keep me grounded. He knows my rhythms, my moods, my silence. But Malik? Malik lights me up. He challenges me. Reminds me I'm still a woman with options."

I leaned back, letting out a long breath. "And Max has no idea?"

"Oh, I would imagine that he suspects," she said, sipping her tea. "That's why he gets so uptight these days. But he's never asked outright, and I've never offered details. We're not exclusive, Joanie. We've never had that talk."

"And you don't feel like that's playing with fire?"

Tremaine tilted her head, thoughtful. "No. I feel like I'm finally living on my terms. I've spent too many years doing things 'the right way'—and what did that ever get me? I'll answer that for you: disappointment and loneliness. This—this is honesty, even if it's messy."

I stared at her, speechless. This was Tremaine: fiercely independent, unapologetically herself, and completely in control. And yet, as she spoke, I couldn't help but wonder if she was as content as she claimed to be.

Tremaine leaned forward, breaking the silence. "But enough about me, Joanie. Let's talk about Jackson. You've been letting that man waste your time, play in your face, and drag you along for years."

"That was different," I shot back. "I knew what it was with him—noncommittal. I was okay with it."

"Until?" Tremaine pressed, raising a skeptical eyebrow.

I hesitated. "Until I started doing some digging. Found his social media and saw him hugged up with some woman in picture after picture. Looked like she could be a damn wife, Tremaine. That's when it hit me: I don't want to be any man's side dish."

"Well damn," Tremaine said, leaning back. "Took you long enough to see the light. But at least you're seeing it now."

"Yeah, and now I'm done with him," I said firmly. "I just need to figure out what's next."

Tremaine's lips curled into a sly smile. "What's next? Oh, honey, you're about to get your groove back, and I'm going to help."

I gave her a wary look. "Help? What are you planning?"

"First," she said, holding up a finger, "we're setting up your profile on some dating sites. Second, we're picking out some new outfits. And third, we're getting you back out there. No excuses."

"Tremaine, I don't know—"

"Joanie, trust me," she interrupted. "It's time. We're going to find you someone who deserves you—or at least someone who knows how to treat you right."

Her determination was infectious, and I found myself nodding. "Alright. Let's do it."

"Cool! Now, that's the Joanie I know and love, okkkaaayyy," Tremaine said with a wink. "Now, finish that tea. We've got work to do. I can't wait for Dana to hear this shit."

Chapter 3

Joanie: An Aha Moment

Once a month, like clockwork, the three of us—Tremaine, Dana, and I—made it a point to reconnect. Girls' night was sacred. We usually hit one of Dallas' trendier spots, drawn by the promise of specialty martinis, citrusy cosmos, or a perfectly salted margarita rim. Truth be told, any excuse for a cocktail—and the chance to swap stories—was good enough for us. How much we drank always depended on the vibe of the place and what kind of week we'd had.

We'd finally put Tremaine's love triangle back in its box—at least for now. I was still curled up on her sectional, nursing what was left of my lavender tea—and to tell the truth, from what Tremaine had recently shared, I was ready for something stronger—when Dana's name lit up Tre's phone.

Our silence was broken by a sudden interruption, Tremaine's phone dinged, signaling a FaceTime call coming in. "It's Dana," she muttered, smirking as she tapped the screen. Dana's face filled the frame, her immaculately styled hair and perfectly arched brows a sharp contrast to Tremaine's laid-back vibe and my casual gallery-worn look.

Dana Franklin, at fifty-seven, my other bestie, often served as our voice of reason. Married to a high-ranking manager at Oncor Electric, where he oversaw the overhead line department, she balanced her own successful career in corporate consulting while maintaining a strong and supportive marriage. Her life seemed perfectly in order, yet she never hesitated to add her unique blend of curiosity and insight to our conversations.

"Hey, girl," Dana greeted, her voice crisp and warm. "I know it's getting close to time for our usual meet-up, and I hadn't heard anything from you two, so I figured I'd better reach out before the time snuck up on us just to get a heads-up on where we're going and to confirm our plans. What're y'all up to? Tremaine, is Joanie there? I checked the Life360 app, so I already know she is. What's going on?"

I rolled my eyes. "Girl! You're worse than my damn momma. We're just sitting around sipping tea and sorting out our messy love lives—you know, the usual."

Dana raised an eyebrow, a knowing smile spreading across her lips. "Messy love lives? Joanie, don't tell me you're still dealing with Jackson's bullshit."

"Actually," I said, sitting up straighter, "I finally decided I'm done with him."

"Finally!" Dana exclaimed, clapping. "I was starting to think you were going to let him string you along forever."

"Well, it's not like your life is entirely drama-free," Tremaine chimed in, leaning closer to the screen. "How's balancing a husband and a career treating you, Mrs. Perfect?"

Dana laughed, brushing an invisible speck off her blouse. "It's not perfect, believe me. But at least my husband isn't juggling three women."

Tremaine and I exchanged a look, stifling our laughter. "Touché," I said, raising my mug of tea in mock salute. "But really, Dana, how do you keep everything together? You make it look so easy."

"Oh, it's anything but," Dana admitted, her tone softening. "Marriage is work. Some days are amazing, and some days, I want to strangle him, but we communicate, we compromise, and we make time for each other. Speaking of which, when are you two going to find some stable men and join me on this side of life?"

"Stable men?" Tremaine scoffed. "Girl, we can't even find men who can commit to dinner, let alone stability."

Dana shook her head, her curiosity shining through her usual practicality. "I don't know how you do it, but I want to hear everything. Tell me about your latest adventures—no holding back."

Tremaine leaned back, smirking. "Oh, you're in for a treat. First, Joanie's going on a dating app."

"A dating app?" Dana nearly dropped her phone. "Joanie, you?"

"Why not?" I said defensively. "It's time."

Dana laughed, her judgment peeking through. "Well, I'm curious to see how that goes. And you, Tremaine? What's your latest escapade?"

Tremaine's grin widened. "Let's see, I'm still in sort of an open relationship, no strings attached with two guys—Max *and* I'm seeing Malik, who's twenty-seven years younger than me."

Dana gasped, her hand flying to her chest. "You're kidding! Tremaine, are you serious?"

"Dead serious," Tremaine replied, unfazed. "And it's fabulous."

"I–I don't even know what to say," Dana stammered. "I mean, Tremaine, twenty-seven years old? Isn't he practically a child?"

"He's forty-three. I said twenty-seven years younger than me," Tremaine corrected. "And no, he's not a child. He's brilliant, funny, and makes me feel alive."

Dana shook her head, her expression a mix of disbelief and judgment. "I don't know how you do it."

"You don't have to," Tremaine said with a wink. "Now, what about you, Dana? What's the secret to your happy marriage?"

Dana hesitated, her confident demeanor faltering for a split second. "Communication," she said finally, but there was something in her tone—something guarded.

Tremaine and I exchanged a glance. "Communication, huh?" I said, leaning closer to the screen. "You sure that's all there is to it?"

Dana's smile tightened. "Of course. Why wouldn't it be?"

"Just curious," Tremaine said, her voice laced with suspicion. "You're holding something back, aren't you?"

Dana waved a hand dismissively. "Don't be ridiculous. Everything's fine. Now, tell me more about these adventures of yours."

But the tension in her voice lingered, and Tremaine and I both knew Dana well enough to know that her ass was holding something back.

Chapter 4

Joanie: Red Flags and New Beginnings

Back at home, I couldn't help but replay the memories of my relationship with Jackson like an old, worn-out movie reel. Where had it all gone so wrong? And how did I miss the signs?

For years, I had convinced myself that Jackson and I were waiting on each other. I didn't want to smother him, and I thought he didn't want to smother me either. I had seen our distance as mutual respect, a way of giving each other space to figure out where we stood. But now, in the quiet of my bedroom, I realized I had been fooling myself.

It was our last visit that opened my eyes. Something about him was different that day. He didn't kiss me when we made love—not even once. He was distant, mechanical, as though he was performing a task he couldn't wait to finish. And then, just when I thought we were reconnecting, he pulled out of me abruptly. I watched in stunned silence as he reached for himself, finishing the act without me. The discomfort that swept over me in that moment was unlike anything I had felt before.

I lay there in bed stunned as he got up and began dressing without a word—no kiss, no lingering touch, nothing. When he left my house, he didn't even say goodbye properly. It was all so odd, so impersonal, but I tried to dismiss it. I told myself he was just tired or distracted.

Then there was the matter of the hotel. He didn't stay with me that night, even though I had offered. Instead, he checked into a hotel. We had planned to meet for dinner, but he called an hour before to cancel, claiming he was too tired and had an early flight out the next morning. That's when the unease really set in. All these little red flags were starting to add up, but I still tried to ignore them.

Until I couldn't.

I was grateful for my girlfriends, so glad I had the kind of friends that I could repeat the same stories to over and over without judgement. I'd finally come clean and told Tremaine what happened, walked her through a most vulnerable moment of my life, piece by piece, it was like trying to make sense of a bad dream. But the truth is, I was still haunted by it. The shock hadn't worn off.

I relived how I'd searched Jackson's social media, the accounts he always kept just out of reach, claiming he wasn't really on there like that. As hard as I tried to shake the memory, I couldn't stop replaying what I'd discovered. What I found stopped me cold.

Picture after picture—him and another woman. Laughing. Hugging. Fingers intertwined like they'd been doing this for a while. One photo showed them at what looked like a family reunion, grinning over paper plates stacked with finger foods and those small, store-bought cupcakes from the chain Smallcakes—the kind with the colorful frosting and too much sprinkles. Another had them on horseback, side by side, looking like a couple straight out of a weekend getaway ad. This wasn't subtle. And it sure as hell wasn't some random post from a forgotten day. It was a storyline—public, polished, and painfully clear. A timeline of shared memories, none of which included me.

She wasn't just some casual fling—she was his significant other. The captions told me everything I needed to know: This man wasn't waiting for me. He had never been waiting for me. He had been living an entirely separate life, one that I had no part in.

From the looks of the photos staring me in my face, he'd been building something real with someone else while I sat there wondering if the pauses in our communication meant he was just busy or just tired. No. He was just taken.

Humiliation. Betrayal. Anger. They all crashed over me like a tidal wave. How could I have been so blind? So naïve?

That night, I blocked his number and every form of communication I had with him. Enough was enough. For the first time in years, I felt a strange sense of relief—like a weight I didn't even realize I was carrying had finally been lifted. But with that relief came a lingering question: What now?

It was Tremaine who pushed me to consider something I never thought I'd do—joining a dating app.

"Joanie, it's time," she said, her tone brooking no argument. "You're not going to meet anyone worthwhile sulking at home. And let's be honest, the gallery isn't exactly a hotspot for eligible bachelors."

I laughed despite myself. "Tremaine, you make it sound so easy. I wouldn't even know where to start."

"That's what I'm here for," she said with a wink. "We're going to set up your profile tonight. Trust me, you're going to love it."

I wasn't so sure about that, but I knew she was right about one thing: It was time to move forward. For too long, I had been stuck in a cycle of hope and disappointment. Maybe, just maybe, this was my chance to break free.

As I sat down to write my profile later that evening, I couldn't help but feel a flicker of excitement. This was new territory—a leap into the unknown. And for the first time in a long while, I felt ready to take it.

The morning sun filtered through my bedroom curtains casting a soft glow over my cozy sanctuary. I reached for my phone, already buzzing on the nightstand. It was a sound I wasn't used to hearing so early, and when I glanced at the screen, my heart skipped a beat: notifications from the dating app. Tremaine hadn't been kidding—this was going to be interesting.

I propped myself up on my pillows, opened the app, and stared at the screen. A little red bubble in the corner of the app icon boasted *12 new notifications*. With a deep breath, I tapped on it.

The first few profiles made me cringe. Men holding up fish, bathroom selfies with terrible lighting, and one guy who clearly had used a picture from twenty years ago—if not longer. "Aw, hell nah," I muttered under my breath, swiping left on one after another.

But just when I was ready to write off the whole experience, a profile caught my eye. His name was Robert. He had a warm smile, poised posture, and the kind of graceful composure and self-assuredness about his eyes that seemed to hold stories. His bio was simple but intriguing: *Retired teacher. Avid traveler. Looking for someone to share life's adventures with.* I paused for a moment, then swiped right.

The next profile wasn't bad either. Marcus, fifty-eight, an architect with a love for jazz and wine tasting. His photo showed him leaning casually against a vineyard fence, dressed in a crisp white linen shirt that screamed confidence without arrogance. Another right swipe.

Then there was James, a former chef who now taught cooking classes. His profile photo showed him in a kitchen, mid-laugh, holding up a tray of what looked like a delicious chocolate cake. "Cooking skills are a bonus," I said aloud, swiping right again.

By the time I had gone through all twelve notifications, I had swiped right on five profiles. Five potential connections, five possibilities. It was more than I had expected for my first dive into the world of online dating.

I set the phone down for a moment, letting the experience sink in. Part of me still felt nervous, unsure if I was really ready for this. But another part—a stronger part—felt a spark of excitement. This was my chance to start fresh, to open myself up to new possibilities.

My phone buzzed again, this time with a message from Tremaine: *How's it going? Have you found anyone interesting yet?*

I laughed, typing back quickly: *A few. I'll keep you posted.*

My phone was lit up like Times Square on New Year's Eve—back-to-back buzzes and I couldn't keep up with each notification. I glanced down to see that Robert and James had both responded. My heart raced a little as I opened Robert's message first. It was short and to the point: *Hi, Joanie. Your profile caught my attention. I'd love to hear about your gallery sometime—art is one of my passions.*

I smiled. A man who liked art? Definitely a good start. I typed back quickly: *Hi, Robert. Thank you! I'd be happy to share more. Are you an artist yourself or just a fan?*

Before I could even open Robert's reply, another notification popped up. James had replied as well: *Joanie, a woman who appreciates good food is already a winner in my book. If you ever want to take a cooking class, I'd be happy to give you a private lesson.*

I laughed out loud, shaking my head. The idea of a private cooking lesson sounded equal parts charming and nerve-wracking.

I replied: *Thank you, James. A private lesson sounds tempting, but you'll have to tell me, what's your signature dish?*

The morning slipped away as I found myself completely engrossed in two alternating conversations. Robert responded with enthusiasm about his favorite art exhibitions, while James detailed a mouthwatering recipe for seafood linguine that had me seriously considering taking him up on his offer.

I'd barely shifted my attention to the TV when another buzz pulled me right back. This time, it was a text from one of my art gallery clients, Veronica. *Joanie, are you available for a private showing this afternoon? I'm looking for a unique piece of artwork for my new condo and would love to see what you have.*

Absolutely, I typed back, already running through my mental inventory. I glanced at the time and realized I shouldn't waste another second in bed swiping and messaging. With a jolt, I swung my legs off the bed and rushed to get ready.

Later that afternoon, I was in the gallery arranging pieces when Veronica arrived. She was younger than most of my clients—mid-thirties at most—and oozed confidence with her sharp blazer and designer heels.

"Joanie, thank you so much for making time," she said, flashing a dazzling smile. "Your gallery is stunning."

"Thank you, Veronica. I'm excited to help you find the perfect pieces," I replied warmly. "What kind of vibe are you looking for?"

"I want something bold," she said, her eyes lighting up as she scanned the room. "Something that makes a statement. My condo is modern, but I want the artwork to bring soul into the space."

"*Hmmm.* Yes. My gallery is my sanctuary," I mused to Veronica as she browsed the South African artwork corner, admiring a piece with bold brushstrokes and vivid hues. "I fell in love with this spot when I first saw the brick on the walls. Like the art on the walls, every brick in here tells a story. When I chose this location in the Bishop Arts District, I knew it had to feel like an extension of me—modern, bold, but with a touch of history."

Veronica nodded, scanning the exposed brick walls and the way they contrasted with the sleek, contemporary furniture. "It's stunning, Joanie. You've created something special here."

"I try," I replied, glancing around the space. "My gallery is a blend of abstract paintings along with modern contemporary with a touch of our rich African-American history. Those hand-carved pieces you're admiring, I handpicked during a trip a few years ago. They are rare finds and are the pride of my collection. But what I cherish most are the works by Dallas' up-and-coming African-American female artists. I have a couple special events showcasing their talent, which has become a passion of mine."

As Veronica continued to peruse the beauty of the gallery, I was equally glad I'd recently had the hardwood floors polished; the floors gleamed with a polished perfection, reflecting the room's quiet charm, casting a glow that made the art come alive. "This place isn't just a business," I continued. "It's my way of connecting with people—through the art, the stories, the emotion it all evokes."

Veronica smiled. "And it shows. This gallery feels like home—to me and for anyone who steps inside."

Yes, I thought. *Intentionally.* My home carried the same elegance. Tremaine had often joked that my gallery was an extension of my own living room, a place where the art and life blended seamlessly.

As we moved from piece to piece, chatting about the inspirations behind each, our conversation took an unexpected turn.

"Relationships are like art, aren't they?" Veronica said suddenly, gesturing to a vibrant abstract piece. "So many layers, so many interpretations."

I chuckled. "I suppose they are. Some are easier to understand than others."

She grinned mischievously. "My husband and I keep things interesting. We're swingers."

I blinked, sure I had misheard her. "Swingers?"

"Yes," she said casually, as though she'd just told me her favorite color. "We have an open arrangement. He has his playdates, as I call them, and I have mine. It keeps things fresh."

I couldn't hide my surprise. "You're...okay with that?"

"Completely," she said, her tone matter-of-fact. "It's about trust. We're honest with each other, and it works for us. You'd be surprised how freeing it is."

I shook my head, trying to process what she was saying. "I don't know if I could ever do that."

"Maybe not," she said with a shrug, "but relationships don't have to fit into one mold. You might want to lighten up a bit, Joanie. Life's too short to follow all the rules."

I tilted my head, trying to mask my surprise. "Well, I can't say I've seen that in today's times. But, Veronica, that's...unique."

She laughed, catching the hint of hesitation in my voice. "Don't worry. I'm not offended if it's not for you. I know it's not everyone's cup of tea."

"I appreciate your honesty," I said carefully. "And believe me, I'm not judging. But for me—where I am in my life—I know I want something different. I'm looking for intimacy and companionship with one person—and let's be clear, a man specifically. That's just where my heart is now."

Veronica shrugged with a knowing smile. "Fair enough. But you might be surprised how liberating it can be. There's no jealousy when there's trust. It's just...freeing."

I nodded thoughtfully. "I can see how it might work for some people, but you know, this isn't really as 'modern' as people think. Open relationships and arrangements like this have been around for centuries. There are stories from the eighteenth century about aristocrats who had official lovers, and in the Harlem Renaissance, some artists and intellectuals lived in unconventional arrangements."

Veronica's eyes widened. "Really? I didn't know that."

"Oh, yes," I said, slipping into gallery educator mode. "People have always found ways to create relationships that work for them, whether society approved or not. But for me, I've always been more of a traditionalist when it comes to love. That's not to say I haven't learned from history, though."

Veronica smiled. "You've got some wisdom in you, Joanie."

"I've just lived long enough to know what I want and what I don't," I replied, laughing. "But I will say this: Relationships are like art. They should inspire you, not leave you feeling like you're missing something."

Veronica paused, her expression softening. "I like that. I'll have to tell my husband that one."

The conversation shifted back to art. Veronica selected two bold pieces that perfectly matched the vibe of her condo. But as she left, her words lingered with me. It wasn't often that someone challenged my perspective so openly—and in such an unexpected way. It left me with something to think about as I closed the gallery for the day, the hum of possibility stirring in the back of my mind. And I was left with more to think about than just art. Hmmm, I thought. Nothing had really changed as it related to relationships, conventionally or unconventionally—only the players had.

Chapter 5

Tremaine: A Day of Reckoning

"How dare you judge me?" I barked into the phone, my voice shaking with frustration. My sister Kim's voice on the other end was as sharp and condescending as ever.

"Tremaine, I'm just saying," Kim replied, her tone dripping with judgment. "Dating a man young enough to be your son? You should be ashamed of yourself."

"Ashamed?" I shot back, pacing the length of my living room. "Who the hell are you to tell me how to live my life? I'm seventy years old. I've earned the right to do what I want with whoever I want. I don't need your approval."

"Seventy or not, it's embarrassing," she retorted. "You're too grown for this nonsense."

I could feel the heat rising in my cheeks. "Listen, just because you've been trapped in a thirty-some-odd-year marriage doesn't mean you get to look down on me. I've never needed a man for anything—not financially, not emotionally, not spiritually. I've built my life on my own terms."

"Maybe that's your problem," she snapped. "Maybe all that independence is why you've never been married."

Her words hit harder than I expected, but I refused to let her see it. "And maybe my independence is the reason I've been successful," I countered. "Maybe it's the reason I've lived a life without regret."

"Tremaine—"

"No," I interrupted, my voice firm. "I don't need this from you. Not today. Not ever."

And with that, I hung up the phone, tossing it onto the couch as I collapsed into the armchair nearby. My chest heaved as I tried to calm the storm of emotions swirling inside me. Frustration. Hurt. Defiance.

I muttered to myself, "Just think if her holier-than-thou ass knew I was seeing Max and all the shit he has going on. She would have a conniption fit!"

The thought brought a bitter smile to my lips. Max, with his cavalier lifestyle and endless ambiguities, was the last thing my judgmental sister needed to hear about. She couldn't handle the idea of me dating Malik—imagine her reaction to Max.

I leaned back in the chair, closing my eyes. The truth was, I was so damn tired of people judging me—my choices, my life, my happiness. If there was one thing I'd learned in my seventy years, it was that you couldn't live for other people's expectations. And I wasn't about to start now.

The sharp trill of my phone broke the silence, snapping me out of my thoughts. I hesitated before picking it up, half-expecting my sister to be calling back for round two, but when I glanced at the screen, it wasn't her name I saw—it was Max.

A knot of unease twisted in my stomach as I stared at the screen. Max rarely called unless it was important—or dramatic. With a deep breath, I swiped to answer.

"Tremaine," his voice came through low and tense, "we need to talk."

My heart sank, the weight of his words pressing heavily on my chest. "What's going on, Max?"

"I'll explain when I see you. Can you come over tonight? Let's say, around seven-ish."

I glanced at the clock, my mind racing. Whatever it was, it didn't sound good. "Alright," I said finally. "I'll be there."

As I hung up, I couldn't shake the feeling that this conversation with Max was going to change everything. For better or worse, I was about to find out.

Chapter 6

Dana: Behind Closed Doors

I adjusted the straps of my silk chemise, glancing at myself in the mirror one last time. The candlelight flickered, casting a warm glow around the bedroom. Soft jazz hummed in the background—I had set the scene perfectly. Tonight, I was determined to rekindle the spark with Trey.

Our home reflected the life we had built together—a sprawling, contemporary masterpiece situated in an affluent Dallas neighborhood with floor-to-ceiling windows that accented our stone-and-stucco exterior. The decor was pristine, almost too perfect, much like the image of our marriage. Neutral tones of cream and taupe filled the space, accented with bold, abstract artwork, pieces Trey and I had collected during our travels. Every detail screamed success, from the carefully arranged bouquets of white lilies to the sleek marble countertops that seemed to sparkle under the recessed lighting.

Friends often commented on how "picture-perfect" our life seemed. They weren't wrong; On the outside, everything appeared seamless. But appearances, as I was beginning to learn, could be deceiving.

I turned to see Trey sitting on the edge of the bed, his fingers pressed against his forehead like he was trying to hold something in—or hold something back. His shoulders sagged under the weight of whatever was on his mind, and his eyes, usually sharp and sure, now carried a shadow of exhaustion I'd never seen in him before. It wasn't just tiredness—it was the kind of weariness that settles deep in the bones.

"Everything okay?" I asked gently, perching on the bed beside him.

He looked up, forcing a smile. "Yeah. Just tired. Long day at the office."

I reached for his hand, squeezing it lightly. "Let's take your mind off work for a while."

Trey nodded, but his gaze shifted, avoiding mine. I leaned in, my lips brushing his neck, and for a moment, I felt him relax under my touch. But as my hands roamed, I sensed the tension returning, his body stiffening.

"Dana..." Trey pulled back, his voice low and strained. "I can't."

My heart sank. "Can't?" I repeated, trying to keep my tone even. "Trey, what's wrong?"

He stood abruptly, pacing the room. "It's not you. It's me," he said, rubbing the back of his neck. "I just...I need some space."

"Space?" I echoed, rising to my feet. "What are you talking about? We've barely spent any time together lately."

"I know," he said, his voice breaking slightly. "I just...I can't do this right now."

Before I could respond, he grabbed his phone from the nightstand and walked out of the room, leaving me standing there, stunned.

I sat back on the bed, my mind racing. Something wasn't adding up. Was it me? Was there someone else? Before this, I'd fought the urge to check his phone when I had the chance. Now, I wrestled with following him out of the room and demanding answers. But I didn't move. Instead, I sat in the silence, the flickering candlelight feeling more oppressive than romantic.

What is happening to us? I thought, clutching the edge of the comforter. For the first time in years, I felt a pang of doubt about our marriage. Was he hiding something? Was there something deeper, something I couldn't see?

The questions lingered as I blew out the candles, leaving the room in darkness. As I slid under the covers alone, my mind replayed the evening's events. Trey's distant demeanor, his reluctance, his hurried departure—they painted a picture I didn't want to believe.

But in my heart, I couldn't shake the feeling that something was off. I had a sick feeling deep inside my gut. Trey and I had been too in sync for me not to know when something was wrong. I swallowed hard, attempting to disregard the lump in my throat, but it was real. The unease gnawed at me, persistent and unrelenting. I needed to know before this thing—whatever it was—escalated out of hand.

Chapter 7

Max: Clear as Mud

I stood in front of the mirror adjusting the collar of my shirt for what felt like the tenth time. My reflection stared back at me calm, composed, but I couldn't deny the storm brewing beneath the surface. Tonight, I had to come clean to Tremaine.

The thought made me pause, a flicker of unease darting across my mind. Honesty wasn't something that came naturally to me, not in relationships. It wasn't that I wanted to lie—I just never gave the full picture. Always a piece, never the whole.

I stepped back, smoothing down my shirt, and allowed my mind to wander. My parents—a nurturing mother who taught me how to be caring and affectionate and a hardworking father who had taught me how to work and generate opportunities for myself—both taught me the value of integrity. Growing up in the Midwest after they migrated from the South, I had watched them struggle and sacrifice. My father worked tirelessly to provide, and my mother's kindness was the glue that held us together. Their marriage was a testament to commitment, but it was also a reminder of what I feared most: the responsibility of love.

Being the first in my family to graduate from college was my proudest moment. I'd built my career from the ground up—grinding through internships, late nights, and deadlines. Journalism was my foundation, but I'd expanded my reach, freelancing as a political analyst for one of Dallas' major news channels. It wasn't always easy, but I'd earned my seat at the table—every byline, every segment, every story. This life? I made it happen, a testament to my determination and drive.

But somewhere along the way, my fear of failure—of not living up to the legacy of my parents' steadfast bond—kept me from committing to anyone. It was easier to keep things casual, to juggle relationships without letting anyone get too close.

That's how I ended up here, a man in his sixties, established and successful, yet still clinging to the illusion of freedom. The truth was, I was scared—scared of being vulnerable. Scared of choosing wrong. And maybe, just maybe, scared of choosing right.

The sharp chime of the doorbell pulled me from my thoughts. My heart kicked up a beat as I glanced at the clock. Tremaine was here.

Straightening my posture, I walked to the door and opened it to find her standing there, every bit as poised and breathtaking as I remembered. Tremaine had a way of commanding attention without trying, her elegance effortless, her confidence palpable.

Seventy or not, she turned heads everywhere she went, and tonight was no exception.

I stepped aside, letting her in. "Tremaine, I appreciate you coming. We need to talk."

"Max," she said, her tone neutral, but her eyes scanning me like she was already bracing for the worse. "Let's get this over with."

"You look and smell sensational as you always do. Come on in." I stepped aside as she brushed passed me.

"Thank you, and no kidding, we do need to talk," she said, settling into the armchair across from the couch. "Go ahead, Max. Say whatever it is you've been rehearsing in that mirror."

I chuckled despite myself. "Fair enough. Look, I want to clear the air about what happened at Joanie's gallery. That...awkwardness shouldn't have happened."

Her brow arched. "Awkwardness? Is that what we're calling it now?"

I let out a slow sigh, rubbing the back of my neck like it might help untangle the mess I'd made. "You're right. It was more than that. And yeah, I'll take the blame. But I really thought I'd been clear from the start—about what this was."

Tremaine folded her arms, her expression tight. "Clear? Max, come on. I've seen clearer mud. You're out here moving like a man with something to hide, but then sitting up talking about it with Joanie—my best friend."

I looked at her, confused. "There's nothing going on with Joanie. You know that."

"I do know that," she shot back. "That's not the point. The point is, why do you feel so damn comfortable laying all your mess at her feet like she's your therapist? You're telling her more than you're telling me—and we're the ones—" she trailed off, catching herself.

"We're not exclusive," I said, quieter now.

"Exactly. So why all the games, Max?" she asked, her voice sharper now. "We have nothing to hide, right? So what's with the smoke and mirrors?"

I opened my mouth but had nothing useful to offer. She wasn't wrong. And suddenly, all that supposed clarity I thought I had? Felt murky as hell.

I felt my jaw tighten. She was right, and we both knew it. "I guess I wasn't as transparent as I thought," I admitted, the words sticking in my throat. "Tremaine, we're grown-ass people. Two adults seeing each other—no titles, no pressure. That's how this started, right? You turn me on—you know that. But I never tried to play you. I thought that was understood."

"Understood or implied?" she repeated, her voice rising. "Max, don't insult me. I've always seen the signs with you. You think I didn't know there were others? Please. But you let me believe—hell, you let *them* believe—that each of us was the only one."

I opened my mouth to respond, but she wasn't done.

"And let me tell you something else," she said, leaning forward. "You being sixty-five and me being seventy is no excuse for you thinking you can play games. You invited me here to be honest?

Fine. Let's both be honest. Since you want to come clean, so will I."

I froze. "What are you talking about, Tremaine?"

She sat back, crossing her legs. "I've been seeing someone else too."

Her words hit me like a slap. I blinked, trying to process what she'd just said. "You...what?"

"His name's Malik," she said, her voice calm but firm. "And before you ask, no, I'm not telling you anything else about him. Not his age, not his background, nothing. Because, frankly, it's none of your business."

My mind raced, but before I could form a coherent thought, she stood. "Now that we're all caught up, Max, what else do you have to say?"

The tension in the room was thick, but before I could respond, I found myself moving toward her. In some weird way, I found myself turned on by her brazenness—or was it I didn't want to be defeated? "Tremaine—"

She held up a hand, but I ignored it. I leaned in, brushing a kiss against her neck, and felt her shudder beneath my touch. One thing I knew for sure was how to turn Tremaine on. At that moment, that was my best ammunition. Whatever anger or frustration she had melted as my lips found hers, and soon, we were tangled in an embrace that was anything but simple.

As we made our way toward the bedroom, one thought kept circling in my mind: We'd done this before—plenty of times. But every time we crossed that emotional line, pretending sex didn't mean more than it should, we made the truth harder to ignore. This wasn't clarity. This was comfort disguised as connection. And somehow, we'd only blurred the lines more than before.

Chapter 8

Trey: Bothered

Traffic was heavy today. I knew I should have left at least fifteen minutes earlier. I looked in the rearview mirror to see an oncoming ambulance coming full speed ahead. I had to pull over to let the emergency vehicle pass. I didn't have a minute to spare. I could see the doctor's office looming just beyond the windshield. My hands gripped the steering wheel for a moment longer than necessary, the weight of what lay ahead settling into my chest. This appointment wasn't just about me—it was about us. About Dana.

As I stepped into the sterile waiting room, I couldn't stop my thoughts from drifting back to her. Dana had been the best thing that had ever happened to me. She saved my life, no question about it. When I met her, I was floundering, unsure of how to pursue my dreams or even where to start. But Dana? She saw the potential in me that I couldn't see in myself. She pushed me, encouraged me, believed in me when no one else did. Within a few months of dating her, I knew she was the one.

We'd always been able to communicate, one of the bedrocks of our marriage. But last night, I'd pushed her away. The look on her face—confusion, hurt—kept replaying in my mind like a broken record. I hoped she wasn't jumping to the wrong conclusions. Dana was the love of my life, and I didn't want to do anything to jeopardize what we had.

But how could I explain this—what I barely understood myself? The shame of it all—the vulnerability I'd been taught to hide at all costs—made my throat tighten. Being a man, at least the way I'd grown up understanding it, meant not showing weakness. I'd seen too many weak men in my childhood—men who made excuses, who gave up, who leaned on others for everything. I'd sworn I'd never be like them.

The nurse called my name, snapping me out of my thoughts. I stood, smoothing down my jacket, and followed her into the examination room. The walls were lined with sterile cabinets, the faint smell of antiseptic in the air. I perched on the edge of the examination table, my hands fidgeting in my lap.

Today, I would find out what was causing my issues. The doctor entered, clipboard in hand, his expression neutral. As he began asking questions, I nodded and answered as best as I could, my heart thudding in my chest. This was it. The moment of truth.

The doctor's pen paused mid-scribble. He looked up, meeting my eyes. "Trey, I think we've identified what's going on, but before I go into detail, I want to assure you, this is treatable."

Relief warred with anxiety. Treatable was good, but it didn't erase the fear. "What exactly is it?" I asked, my voice barely above a whisper.

The doctor began explaining, but his words blurred as my mind raced ahead. Would this change everything? Could Dana and I work through this? Did I even have the courage to tell her?

I blinked, forcing myself to focus on the doctor's words as he outlined the next steps. As I listened, a thought nagged at the back of my mind, unshakable and insistent: *Was it already too late?*

Chapter 9

Joanie: A Leap of Faith

The soft chime of the gallery's clock signaled the end of another long day. I stood by the counter, carefully wrapping the last painting in brown kraft paper, the scent of fresh coffee still lingering faintly in the air. Business had been steady, and for that, I was grateful. But tonight, my mind was elsewhere.

As I gathered my things, my phone pinged. I glanced at the screen, my heart skipping a beat when I saw his name: Robert. We'd been chatting for weeks now on the dating app, exchanging everything from lighthearted banter to surprisingly deep conversations. Yet, I hadn't mustered the courage to meet him in person.

Until tonight.

Hey, Joanie, his message began. *Any chance I can convince you to grab a drink with me? I know a great jazz spot in Dallas. Very public, very neutral, and very good music.*

I hesitated, my fingers hovering over the keyboard. Meeting someone from a dating app felt like uncharted territory, and the thought of stepping outside my comfort zone made my stomach twist. But there was something about Robert—his wit, his warmth, his apparent sincerity—that made me want to take the chance.

Alright, I typed back, my pulse quickening. *What time?*

His response was immediate: *7 PM. I'll text you the address.*

I swallowed hard, nervous energy coursing through me. Could I really do this? Before I could second-guess myself, my phone buzzed again. This time, it was Tremaine.

"Girl, you won't believe what I've done," she said the moment I answered.

"Tremaine," I said with a laugh, "what now?"

"I fell into Max's arms, that's what," she said, her voice a mix of frustration and regret. "After everything, I let myself get swept up in his charm. I let that muthafucka woo, woo, woo, me. I can't believe I let it happen."

"Tremaine," I said softly, "you're human. Don't be so hard on yourself."

"I know," she admitted, "but it's just...I'm so mad at myself. I knew better. And now, I have to figure out what the hell I'm going to do about him."

We talked for a while, her words echoing the inner turmoil I'd felt so many times before. By the time we hung up, I felt a strange sense of resolve. If Tremaine could face her fears and confront her choices, so could I.

At six forty-five, I stood in front of my closet, rifling through dresses until I found a simple black number that felt just right—not too flashy, not too casual. I paired it with a pair of heels and a silver necklace, then took a deep breath before heading out the door.

The jazz spot was just as Robert had described—cozy, vibrant, and alive with the sound of saxophones and upright bass. As I walked in, I scanned the room until they landed on him. He stood near the bar, a warm smile spreading across his face as he spotted me.

"Joanie," he said, extending a hand. "I'm so glad you came."

"Me too," I said, my voice steadier than I felt.

We found a table near the stage, the sounds of Boney James providing the perfect backdrop as we talked. He leaned in, his voice low and inviting as he shared stories of his travels, his favorite jazz albums, and his love for art. Every word felt genuine, and I found myself smiling more than I had in years.

"So, tell me, Joanie," he said, his eyes sparkling under the dim light, "what inspired you to open your gallery?"

I hesitated, surprised by how easily he made me want to share. "It's a long story," I began, then paused, "but let's just say, art has always been my sanctuary. It's where I find peace, even when life gets messy."

"I can see that," he said, his gaze thoughtful. "You have a way of carrying yourself, like someone who's found her place in the world."

His words caught me off guard, and for a moment, I felt seen in a way I hadn't in a long time. The conversation continued. The tension I'd been carrying seemed to melt away.

After an hour of easy conversation, the band began playing a slower tune by Avery Sunshine, and Robert extended his hand. "Would you like to dance?"

I hesitated, then placed my hand in his. "Why not?"

The music enveloped us as we swayed to the rhythm. For the first time in ages, I felt free, untethered by the past. The night wound down. I realized this was more than just a first meeting—it was the start of something new.

But in the back of my mind, a question lingered: Was I truly ready for what came next?

Chapter 10

Dana: Searching for Answers

I sat on the edge of my bed, staring at my phone like it held all the answers I couldn't seem to find. Trey's distance had left me reeling, and no matter how much I tried to rationalize it, the doubt gnawed at me. Was it something I'd done—or worse, was there someone else?

I tossed the phone onto the comforter and leaned forward, resting my head in my hands. This wasn't like us. But now, the silence between us was deafening.

I couldn't stop my thoughts from spiraling. How did we get here? I replayed our recent interactions, searching for any clue I might have missed. His distance wasn't just physical—it was emotional, like a wall had been built between us, and I didn't know how to tear it down.

Memories of how we used to be flooded my mind. When we first met, I was presenting at a marketing conference, and he was speaking about sustainable business. He had this charm about him, a confidence that drew me in instantly. By the end of that weekend, I knew he was someone special. We built a life together, a partnership rooted in trust and mutual respect, so why did it feel like we were crumbling now?

I thought about the nights we'd stayed up late talking about our dreams, our fears, our plans for the future. Where had that version of us gone? Were we still in there somewhere, buried beneath the weight of time and unspoken words?

My mother's voice echoed in my head, her words as clear as if she were sitting beside me. *"Dana, don't try to fit in with your girlfriends just because they don't have a man. You do, so act accordingly. You don't have to be judgmental, but know how to treat your man and your relationship."* She'd instilled in me the importance of nurturing what you have, of not letting outside influences cloud your perspective, but what was I supposed to do when I felt like I was the only one fighting for us?

I sighed and picked up my phone again, scrolling through old photos of Trey and me. There we were at a friend's wedding, dancing like no one else was in the room. Another picture showed us laughing on a beach, his arm around my shoulders, the sun setting behind us. Those moments felt like a lifetime ago.

And then, there was that little voice—the one I tried to silence but couldn't ignore. *What if I'm fighting a battle Trey had already decided to surrender?*

I didn't want to believe it, but the thought wouldn't leave me alone. The doubt, the fear, the aching sense of loss—it all coiled tightly around my heart, making it hard to breathe. I wasn't ready to let go, but I couldn't keep holding on to something that felt so tenuous.

Finally, I couldn't take it anymore. I opened my messages and typed: *We need to talk. Tonight. No excuses.*

I stared at the text for a long moment before hitting send. My stomach churned as I imagined how the conversation might go. Would he open up, or would he retreat farther into himself, leaving me with even more questions?

All I knew was that I couldn't keep living in this limbo. Trey was the love of my life, and I wasn't ready to give up on us. But as I sat there, waiting for his response, a tiny voice in the back of my mind whispered the one thing I was most afraid to admit: *What if it's already too late?*

The ping of my phone startled me, and my heart leaped into my throat. His name flashed across the screen, and for a moment, I couldn't bring myself to open the message. I took a deep breath, bracing myself, and tapped the notification.

Let's talk, it read. *I'll be home by 7.*

I exhaled shakily, but the knot in my chest didn't loosen. This was it. Tonight, I would find out whether we still had a future—or if I'd been clinging to a memory of what once was.

Chapter 11

Joanie: Standards and Realizations

The house was silent except for the faint hum of the fridge in the kitchen. I sat on the couch, my legs tucked beneath me, a glass of Prosecco balanced in one hand. The evening had been pleasant—Robert had been charming and thoughtful, and for a moment, I allowed myself to believe that maybe, just maybe, this dating app experiment wasn't a total waste of time.

But now, as the warmth of the sparkling wine settled over me, my thoughts wandered to the past. To Jackson.

I set the glass down on the coffee table and sighed, leaning back into the cushions. Jackson. What a mess that had been. I couldn't help but hear my own voice echoing back at me from a conversation I'd had with the girls months ago. "He'll have to let me go," I'd joked, laughing as I swirled my drink, "because his dick is too good to let go."

The memory made me cringe. Had that been all it ever was? Had I really allowed myself to settle for crumbs and convince myself it was a feast? My ego had taken a brutal hit when I discovered the real reason Jackson had always been so vague, so elusive.

I could still remember the moment I saw it—the pictures, one after another, of him with another woman. And not just casual snapshots either. No, these were the kind of photos that told a story, that radiated intimacy. The way he grinned, his arm draped possessively around her waist, his eyes lighting up in a way I had never seen before. That large, beaming smile. Not once had he ever looked at me like that. Hell, we had never even taken a single selfie together.

It had felt like a punch to the gut. A wave of nausea rolled over me so strong, I had to sit down. No matter how much I blinked, I couldn't unsee what I had seen.

But now, as I sat in my own space, staring at the shadows dancing on the wall, I had to ask myself the hard question: Did Jackson play me, or had I played myself?

The truth was painful, but undeniable. I had lowered my standards for the illusion of connection, for fleeting companionship that had left me feeling emptier than before. Jackson and I had had nothing real. Nothing substantial. And yet, I'd clung to him as if he were the last lifeboat on a sinking ship. And I was tired.

I ran a hand through my hair, shaking my head at my own reflection in the darkened window. "Never again," I muttered to myself. "I'm done with lowering my standards."

It wasn't just about Jackson. It was about all of them—the string of men who had come and gone, each one chipping away at my sense of self-worth, at my belief in what I truly deserved. Tonight, as I sat alone in my quiet house, I made a vow to myself: I would no longer settle. Not for charm, not for potential, and certainly not for a warm body to fill the silence.

For the first time in a long time, I felt a flicker of hope. Hope that maybe, just maybe, there was something better waiting for me. Someone better. But even if there wasn't, I was determined to be enough for myself.

I walked to my bar. This time I poured me a shot of Don Julio tequila. I picked up my glass and took a long gulp, letting the drink warm me from the inside out. The night was young, and my journey was far from over.

Chapter 12

Tremaine: Unraveled Plans

I paced my living room, phone in hand, trying to shake the frustration bubbling up inside me. I'd called Joanie earlier to vent about the mess with Max, but she was busy. That left me alone with my thoughts—never a good place to be.

How could I let this happen? Again. I hated myself for falling back into Max's arms, for believing even for a second that things could be different this time. After everything he'd done, after all the signs I'd chosen to ignore, I still let him get to me.

I stopped pacing and sank onto the couch, staring at my phone like it might hold the answers I needed. The screen lit up with a message from Malik: *What's up, gorgeous? You free tonight?*

I rolled my eyes. Malik and his impeccable timing. Normally, I'd be down for a late-night rendezvous—no strings, no expectations—but tonight, the message just irritated me. It felt shallow, a distraction from the storm raging inside me.

At first, I set the phone down without replying and leaned back, closing my eyes. My thoughts drifted to Max and the way he looked at me that night at Joanie's gallery. It wasn't just awkward; it was humiliating. And yet, I had let him smooth talk his way back into my space, and I was back in his bed. I hated the part of me that still craved his attention, his charm, his touch.

What is wrong with me? I thought. *Why do I keep lowering my standards for fleeting companionship?*

The truth hit me like a slap. I'd always prided myself on being a grown woman—someone who knew what she wanted and wouldn't settle for less. But here I was, compromising, settling, pretending I didn't see the red flags because I didn't want to be alone.

My mother's voice echoed in my head: *"Tremaine, never let loneliness make you forget your standards. A man can only do to you what you allow."* She'd said it to me so many times growing up, drilling it into my head like a mantra. And for most of my life, I'd lived by those words. So why was I forgetting them now?

I picked up my phone again and stared at Malik's message. And without any further thought, I replied, *Come over.*

Twenty minutes later, Malik was at my door, flashing that cocky grin I knew so well. He pulled me into his arms without hesitation, his familiar scent wrapping around me. For a moment, I let myself lean into him, craving the comfort of his touch.

"You look amazing," he murmured, his lips grazing my ear. "I missed you."

I managed a small smile. "Missed you too."

We didn't waste much time talking. Malik had always been good at making me forget, at least for a little while. His touch, his energy—it was exactly what I thought I needed. The fire was there, the passion undeniable. But somewhere in the middle of it all, I felt...disconnected. The release I was chasing stayed just out of reach, leaving me emptier than before.

When it was over, Malik lay beside me, his arm draped lazily across my waist. "Damn, Tremaine," he said with a satisfied smirk. "You're something else."

I turned away, a wave of regret crashing over me. My chest felt tight, and my thoughts were louder than ever. I sat up, pulling the sheet around me like a shield. "Malik," I said softly, "I think you should go."

He frowned, propping himself up on one elbow. "What? Why? What about a round two?"

"I'm not feeling well," I lied, avoiding his gaze. "I think I just need to be alone."

"Tremaine," he said, sitting up fully now, "this isn't like you. What's going on?"

"Nothing," I snapped, harsher than I intended. "I just...I have a headache, alright? Please."

He studied me for a moment, his concern evident, but he didn't push. "Alright...cool," he said quietly, getting out of bed. "Feel better, okay?"

I nodded, watching his chiseled physique as he dressed and walked to the door. The sound of it closing behind him felt like both a relief and a slap in the face. Alone again, the weight of my choices pressed down on me.

I wrapped myself in my robe and made my way to the bathroom, avoiding my reflection in the mirror. Sitting on the cold tile floor, I pulled my knees to my chest and let the tears come—not for Malik, not even for Max, but for me. For the woman I used to be, the one I was desperate to find again.

I didn't know how to fix this chaos I'd made of my life, but one thing was clear: Something had to change. And soon.

Chapter 13

Joanie: Basking in Glory

Since my experience with Robert, I had a newfound confidence in meeting my online acquaintances in person. I stood in front of my mirror, carefully applying the final touches to my lipstick. My heart raced in a way that felt both thrilling and nerve-wracking. Tonight, I was meeting James. We'd been texting for days, our conversations flowing with an ease I hadn't expected. Now, it was time to see if the connection translated in person.

My gallery was a reflection of me—sophisticated, bold, and unapologetically mine. Tucked into the heart of the Bishop Arts District, it struck that balance I'd always loved: where contemporary edge met quiet history. The exposed brick walls carried a warmth that softened the sleek, modern lines of the space, while vibrant abstracts lit up the room with color and movement. A corner near the back held a special place in my heart—South

African pieces I'd collected on a trip years ago, each one layered with memory.

What mattered most to me, though, were the works by emerging African-American women artists from Dallas. Their voices, their vision—I made sure they had a home on these walls. Every curated showing was a chance to spotlight them, to say we belong in this space too.

Even the polished floors, glowing under soft track lighting, felt intentional. Minimalist decor kept the focus where it should be—on the art. On the story. On the power of what's been created.

The energy inside the gallery often mirrored mine—alive, intuitive, never trying too hard. I knew how to make people feel seen, understood. Years of working with Dallas' choosiest collectors had taught me that much. But it wasn't just business. It was personal. Art had always been my anchor.

I used to joke the gallery was just an extension of my living room—and in many ways, it was. Home bled into work, and work into life. Everything overlapped in soft, deliberate brushstrokes. But tonight, none of that was on my mind. Not the gallery. Not Jackson. Not the carefully curated image I maintained.

Tonight was about me.

When I arrived at the address James had sent, my breath caught. A small airfield stretched before me, the setting sun casting golden hues across the tarmac. James stood near a sleek helicopter, his broad smile instantly putting me at ease.

"Joanie," he said, extending a hand to help me out of my car. "I thought we'd do something memorable tonight."

I blinked, taken aback. "A helicopter ride?"

He chuckled. "I figured the Dallas skyline deserves to be seen from a proper vantage point. What do you think?"

For a moment, I was speechless. No one had ever planned something so elaborate for me. I nodded, excitement bubbling over. "I think it's incredible."

The pilot greeted us, and soon, we were soaring above the city. The skyline twinkled beneath us, a breathtaking tapestry of lights against the darkening sky. James leaned closer; his voice soft but audible over the hum of the rotor.

"You deserve experiences like this," he said, his eyes locking with mine. "And more."

A warmth spread through my chest, a mixture of awe and something deeper. The helicopter circled the city. I allowed myself to be fully present, soaking in every detail—the sparkle of the lighted buildings, the magnificent Margaret McDermott Bridge, the Margaret Hunt Hill Bridge, the Cotton Bowl, and Texas State Ferris Wheel, all set against the serenity of the moment, as well as the undeniable chemistry between us.

When we landed, James guided me to a drop-off at Reunion Tower, where a small catered dinner awaited. We talked for hours, laughter and meaningful conversation weaving a connection that felt almost surreal.

Hours later, I couldn't help but reflect on my earlier vow of abstinence. For the first time in a long while, I felt no need to rush anything. This moment—this connection—was enough, and I intended to savor every moment of it.

As we said our goodbyes, James brought his face close, pressing a light kiss to my cheek. "Let me know when you're ready for our next adventure," he said with a wink.

I watched him walk away, a smile tugging at my lips. Our date left me feeling hopeful. But as I drove home, my phone buzzed with a notification. I glanced at the screen, my heart skipping a beat. It was a message from Robert.

Thinking about you, Joanie. Can't wait to see you again.

The warmth from the evening lingered, but now, a flicker of doubt crept in. Was I ready to juggle two connections? And more importantly, was I ready for what came next?

Chapter 14

Joanie: The Meetup

The lounge in The Colony was the epitome of upscale relaxation. Warm ambient lighting bounced off the sleek mahogany bar, and the gentle hum of conversation mixed with the soulful sounds of Avery Sunshine's silky voice drifting from the speakers. A rotation of tracks by Kem and Stokely added to the atmosphere, wrapping the space in an intimate, romantic vibe. The menu boasted themed cocktails with names like Soul Serenade and Velvet Touch, paired with plates of upscale soul food—fried green tomatoes, Cajun shrimp skewers, and chicken and waffle bites served with honey-drizzled perfection.

The three of us—Tremaine, Dana, and I—occupied a corner booth near the back, the plush leather seats framing our lively conversation. Tremaine was in the middle of a story, her silver locs catching the soft glow of the pendant lights as she gestured animatedly.

"I'm telling you, this place has it all," I said, waving my hand at the spread before us. "Good food, good drinks, good vibes."

"And a nice view," Tremaine added slyly, nodding toward a young man seated at the bar. He had been stealing glances in her direction all evening.

I followed her gaze and smirked. "Girl, if you don't stop being a magnet for these man-children."

Dana nearly choked on her drink, laughing. "Tremaine, you really do have a type. Do they still call you Professor Robinson, or do you make them call you something else now?"

Tremaine rolled her eyes, but the corner of her mouth lifted in amusement. "Don't hate the player, ladies. And for the record, I'm not interested tonight. Let the boy wonder."

"Uh-huh," I teased. "You better watch out. He might write his dissertation on you."

The laughter rolled easily, the kind that felt like a balm after long days and lingering stress. But as the conversation turned more serious, the energy at the table shifted slightly.

"So, Dana," Tremaine began, leaning back in her seat, "you've been real quiet tonight. What's going on?"

Dana hesitated, her fingers tracing the stem of her glass. "It's Trey," she admitted finally. "The other night it happened again."

"What happened again?" I asked gently, setting my drink down.

Dana sighed, glancing around the room as if searching for the right words. "He just...he shut down. We were supposed to have this perfect night—candles, music, everything. But he couldn't.

He walked out of the room, said he needed space. It's happened more than once now."

Tremaine tilted her head, her expression unreadable. "And you haven't talked about it?"

"We're supposed to," Dana said, her voice tinged with frustration, "but it hasn't happened yet. I don't know. Maybe I'm overthinking it. Maybe it's work stress or something."

I reached across the table, giving Dana's hand a reassuring squeeze. "Dana, you've been married for years. You two have been through so much together. There's no way Trey would hurt you."

"Joanie's right," Tremaine added. "You're jumping to conclusions. Don't let your mind get ahead of the facts."

Dana nodded slowly, though the uncertainty lingered in her eyes. "You're probably right. I just... Sometimes it feels like I'm waiting for the other shoe to drop."

"Well," I said with a small smile, "just don't wait too long to talk to him. Communication is everything, right?"

Dana nodded again but quickly shifted gears. "Alright. Enough about me. What's going on with you two?"

"Oh, honey," Tremaine said, her grin returning. "Max is still his usual charming self, and Malik... Well, let's just say that man has a PhD in making me laugh."

I raised an eyebrow. "Laugh? Is that what they're calling it now?"

"Don't start with me, Joanie," Tremaine shot back playfully. "I'm living my life, and I make no apologies."

Dana shook her head, a mix of curiosity and envy flickering in her eyes. "I don't know how you do it, Tremaine. Balancing all of that... Doesn't it get exhausting?"

"Life's exhausting," Tremaine said with a shrug. "Might as well enjoy it."

I leaned in, a mischievous glint in my eye. "Yeah, out of the three of us, it's the seventy-year-old getting more head—"

I hadn't completed my sentence when Tremaine jokingly interrupted me, "Now, now, brown cow."

"Girl, will you please get your mind out of the gutter? What I was trying to say was, getting more attention, *heads turned*, getting chose, and checking you out than either of us," I motioned my pointed finger between me and Dana. "Speaking of enjoying life, I had the experience of a lifetime the other night with James."

"Oh. We're listening," Tremaine said, her interest piqued.

I recounted the helicopter ride, the skyline views, and the elegant dinner at Reunion Tower. "It was incredible," I concluded, "but I'm still cautious. After Jackson, it's hard not to be."

"Speaking of Jackson," Dana interjected, her tone careful, "have you heard from him?"

"No, ma'am," I said firmly, "and I hope he's living his best life. What I know is everything ain't for everybody. And in my opinion, what he did to me was completely foul, but life goes on, and I wish him well in his future endeavors. I just know I don't want to speak with him, see him, or have that type of energy in my life ever again. I've moved on."

The table fell silent for a moment before Tremaine raised her glass. "To moving on."

"To moving on," Dana and I echoed, clinking our glasses.

Dana sighed, leaning back. "Joanie, I know you're feeling this online dating thing, but are you sure it's safe?"

I shrugged, my confidence returning. "Nothing in life is without risk, Dana. And honestly, what do I have to lose?"

Dana tilted her head in agreement, though her lips pouted in a smile. "Good point. I just hope you know what you're doing."

I raised my glass again with a smirk. "Here's to finding out."

The three of us laughed, our conversation winding down. The music shifted to another soulful track. A good time had been had by us all. We hugged and parted ways, each heading to our cars under the glow of the lounge's marquee lights. But as I drove through the quiet streets, I couldn't shake the feeling of too many unanswered questions hanging in the air. Knowing my girls as well as I do, I'm certain we were all driving to our destinations silent and lost in thought, each of us wondering what twists and turns lay ahead in our lives.

Chapter 15

Joanie: Reflection and Self-Care

The sunlight filtered through the sheer curtains of my bedroom as I stood in front of the mirror, brushing a final stroke of blush across my cheeks. My mornings had become a ritual of focus and preparation, a way to center myself before heading to the gallery, which had always been my haven—a space where creativity and connection came alive. Lately, I'd noticed the weight of expectations creeping into its walls, especially with the buzz surrounding my next showcase.

I glanced over at my neatly arranged planner on the desk. Today was packed with meetings, emails, and preparing for the arrival of a new South African collection I'd been eagerly anticipating. The rhythm of my life was steady, predictable even, but I couldn't shake the feeling that a shift was coming, one that I wasn't entirely prepared for.

Just as I reached for my bag, my phone buzzed on the dresser. It was a text from Robert.

Good morning, Joanie. Hope your day is off to a beautiful start. I was wondering if you'd be free for an outing sometime in our near foreseeable future. I have an idea I think you'll love.

My lips curved into a smile as I read his message. Robert's thoughtful demeanor always managed to make me pause. He had a way of being intentional with his words, which was refreshing after the chaos I'd endured with Jackson. Still, a part of me hesitated. I wasn't sure if I was ready to let my guard down again.

I typed back: *Good morning, Robert. How thoughtful of you to think of me. Why yes, I'm interested. After I get to the gallery, I'll check my availability and get back with you.*

His response came quickly: *There's a showing of the Kinsey African American Art & History Collection at the Holocaust Museum in Houston. I'd love to go with you. It's an incredible exhibit—you might even know it.*

My heart skipped a beat. The Kinsey Collection was one of the most renowned private holdings of African American art and artifacts. I'd met Bernard and Shirley Kinsey years ago during a girls' trip to Jamaica, and their passion for preserving history had left a lasting impression on me. This wasn't just any outing—this was a chance to immerse myself in something I deeply cherished.

I couldn't help but laugh softly to myself as I typed back: *I actually met the Kinseys once! This sounds perfect. Let's plan for it. My only caveat is the exhibit is in Houston, a four-hour drive from Dallas.*

So, I wonder to myself, does that mean an overnighter with a man I barely know? Already? *Hmmm.* I'd have to give that some serious thought.

Almost as if he sensed my hesitation, Robert followed up with another message: *No worries, Joanie. I'll make sure you have your own private hotel accommodations. No hidden agenda—just an evening of two avid art lovers enjoying the experience. Also, the exhibit will be there for the next few months, so check your schedule and let me know what works best for you.*

I smiled, feeling my reservations ease. His sensitivity to my comfort wasn't something I was used to. Sliding my phone into my bag, I felt a renewed sense of excitement for the day ahead. The idea of sharing this experience with Robert was both thrilling and comforting. He had a way of making me feel seen in a way I hadn't in years.

The thought lingered as I drove to the gallery, the morning sun casting golden rays across the city streets. As I stepped inside, the familiar scent of polished wood and faint traces of paint greeted me, grounding me instantly. The gallery was my sanctuary, the place where I felt most like myself. But even here, the flutter of anticipation for what was to come hummed in my chest. For the first time in a long while, the future felt like a blank canvas, waiting for me to make the first bold stroke.

Chapter 16

Tremaine: A Morning Disruption

The sun was just peeking over the horizon as I laced up my sneakers and stepped onto my porch, ready for my morning run. The air was crisp, carrying the faint scent of dew and wildflowers. It was the perfect start to the day—or at least, it should have been.

But just as I took my first stretch, a familiar car pulled up in front of my house. Malik. My heart sank, not because I wasn't glad to see him—he was always a sight to behold—but because this was unexpected. Unannounced. Not like him at all.

He stepped out of his car holding a cup of my favorite Starbucks mojo like a peace offering. His easy grin was disarming, but I wasn't about to let him off that easy. I crossed my arms and leaned against the porch rail, waiting for him to speak.

"Good morning, gorgeous," he said, holding out the cup. "Thought I'd bring you something to start your day."

"Malik," I began, my tone measured. "What are you doing here? You didn't call. Don't tell me you're catching feelings. We're not exclusive remember?"

He looked taken aback, then shrugged. "I thought I'd surprise you. Is that a crime?"

"Not a crime," I said, taking the cup but not sipping. "But it's not like you. We've always had an understanding. No surprises, no expectations."

"Yeah, I know," he said, scratching the back of his neck, "but...about the other night... I just wanted to check in. You left me...confused."

I raised an eyebrow. "Confused? How so? I asked you to leave because I wasn't feeling well. What's there to be confused about?"

He hesitated, his confidence faltering for a moment. "Look, Tremaine, I know we're not exclusive, but I've never had you ask me to leave like that before. It was...different. I just want to make sure we're good."

I sighed, stepping down from the porch to stand directly in front of him. "Malik, you know we're good. You're making a big deal out of nothing. But let's be real here—are you jealous? Because that's not what either of us signed up for, remember?"

His eyes narrowed slightly; his pride clearly stung. "Jealous? No, I'm not jealous. I just think—"

"You just think what?" I interrupted, my tone sharper now. "You're forty-three, Malik. Let's not play games. If you're catching feelings, just say so. Don't stand here acting like I did something wrong when we both agreed this wasn't about commitment. "

He opened his mouth to respond, but nothing came out. Instead, he looked away, his jaw tightening. It was then that I saw it—something unspoken lingering in his expression. It wasn't just bruised ego; it was something deeper.

"You're not telling me everything," I said, my voice softer now. "What's going on, Malik?"

He shook his head, letting out a hollow laugh. "Nothing. You're right. I'm overthinking it. Look, enjoy your drink. I'll let you get back to your run."

But as he turned to leave, I couldn't shake the feeling that he wasn't being honest. His actions said one thing, but his body language screamed another. Watching him drive away, I felt a knot form in my stomach. Something about this wasn't sitting right.

I took a long sip of my coffee, letting the warmth soothe my nerves, but my thoughts remained tangled. Malik was starting to cross lines we'd never drawn, and I wasn't sure what that meant for us—or for me.

Chapter 17

Dana: A Growing Divide

The storm last night had been relentless, with howling winds and torrential rain battering the windows. It was the kind of weather that made sleep nearly impossible, and yet, at some point, exhaustion had won out. I woke to the gray light of morning filtering through the clouds, illuminating the empty side of the bed where Trey should have been. My phone buzzed on the nightstand, and I groggily reached for it. A text from Trey flashed on the screen.

Stayed over at work. Severe weather kept us tied up. Be home soon.

I sighed, sitting up and scratching my scalp through my silk hair bonnet. Of course, work. Trey's role as a manager at Oncor often demanded long hours, especially during stormy weather. I couldn't blame him—it was his job to ensure linemen and technicians were safe and the city's power stayed on. But still, disappointment settled over me like a heavy blanket. He had promised we'd talk last night, I'd stayed up waiting as long as

I could before eventually dozing off on the sofa. After a while, I dragged myself to bed in the wee hours of the morning, still half-asleep and disappointed.

Shaking off the remnants of sleep, I slid out of bed and headed to the bathroom to prepare for the day. Just as I reached for the shower knob, the sound of our bedroom door opening startled me.

"Dana?" Trey's voice echoed through the room.

I wrapped my robe tighter and stepped out of the bathroom into our adjoining bedroom, finding him standing by the door, his rain-soaked jacket draped over one arm. His face looked weary; his salt-and-pepper hair disheveled. But as soon as he saw me, something in his expression shifted. Before I could say a word, he crossed the space between us and pulled me into a tight embrace.

"I'm so sorry," he murmured into my hair. "I've been carrying this for too long."

My heart raced. This was it. My worst fear. Was he about to confess?

I pulled back just enough to look into his eyes, my voice trembling. "Trey, what is it? Please, just tell me."

He swallowed hard, his jaw tightening. "I didn't want to burden you, Dana. You've always been my rock, my everything. I didn't know how to... I didn't know how to tell you."

My stomach tightened as he stepped away, his hands trembling slightly as he reached into the side drawer of the console by the door. He hesitated for a moment, then pulled out a folder and handed it to me.

"This," he said, his voice raw, barely above a whisper. "This is what I've been dealing with."

With unsteady fingers, I opened the folder, my eyes skimming over the papers inside. At first, the words blurred, but then they sharpened into something undeniable: *Diagnosis...Summary...Pathology Results...Gleason Score...Prostate Cancer...Staging Information...Imaging Reports (MRI, CT Scan)...Treatment Options...Possible Side Effects.*

A chill washed over me. My breath caught in my throat as I looked up, my vision blurred with tears.

"Trey..." My voice cracked. "Why didn't you tell me?"

"Because I didn't want you to see me like this," he admitted, his voice heavy with emotion. "I didn't want you to see me as less of a man."

"Less of a man?" I repeated, shaking my head. "Trey, you're my husband, my partner. We're supposed to go through these things together. I can't believe you've been carrying this alone."

He sank onto the edge of the bed, his shoulders slumping. "I've been so afraid, Dana—afraid of losing you, afraid of...what this means for us."

I knelt in front of him, taking his hands in mine. "Trey, listen to me: Whatever this is, we're going to face it together. You don't have to go through this alone anymore. Do you hear me?"

He nodded, tears streaming down his face. For the first time in months, it felt like a wall between us had been shattered. But even as relief washed over me, a new kind of fear took its place. What did this mean for our future? For our intimacy? For us?

I pressed a kiss to his hands, vowing silently to be the strength he needed. But deep down, I knew this was just the beginning of a long road ahead. As we parted ways—Trey went to shower, I headed to our kitchen to prepare a nice breakfast of bacon, grits, eggs and cheese, toast, and agave—I couldn't stop thinking about Trey. His confession about his health had opened the door to so many questions, but there was one I couldn't shake: *What else hasn't he told me?*

In all the thirty-plus years we'd been together, Trey and I never kept anything from each other, at least not that I knew of. Just as my eyes started to close, Trey's phone, sitting on the kitchen island, lit up with a notification. The name on the screen wasn't familiar, and the message preview was cryptic: *Let's meet again soon. I'm here for you anytime you need me.*

Chapter 18

Joanie: Trust Your Gut

The restaurant was alive with energy, a modern yet cozy spot in Uptown Dallas with high ceilings, industrial lighting, and walls adorned with local artwork. The three of us—Dana, Tremaine, and I—settled into a corner booth, one of our favorite spots at this particular location during our monthly meet-ups. The scent of truffle fries and freshly grilled salmon wafted through the air as a playlist of smooth old-school R & B music hummed softly in the background.

"So," Tremaine began, swirling the olive in her martini glass. "Let's get into it. Joanie, since our last meeting, you've been entertaining not one, but two online suitors? Girl, you're an online dating pro. Tell us what's been going on?"

I couldn't help but laugh as I rolled my eyes. "It's not what you think. I'm just exploring my options. I mean, isn't that what dating is about?"

"Options?" Tremaine smirked. "Sounds like you're doing what men have been doing to us for years. Have some fun, but don't take it so seriously. You know online dating is very similar to social media. Everyone is not who or what they seem. Everyone shows up as their best representative."

I shot her a playful glare. "First of all, let's be clear: I'm not sleeping with either of them. I've made it very upfront to both James and Robert that I'm taking things slow. If anything, I've been overly cautious."

"Wait," Tremaine said, leaning forward. "You're already paused taking any more hits off the app, right? I mean with all that you have going on, I don't know if you can fit any more into your already busy schedule. So, what's the deal?"

I nodded. "Yeah, I got off the app for now. Between work and spending time with them, I haven't had the energy to keep up with anyone else. But..." She hesitated, tapping her finger against the edge of her glass.

"But what?" Tremaine pressed.

"There's a red flag with Robert," I admitted. "In one conversation, he mentioned having one son who he is heavily involved with and being married once, but in another conversation we were having, he slipped and said 'my sons.' Plural. It threw me off, so I did some digging. Fast People Search, Facebook—everything. Turns out, he's been married twice, and he has two sons."

"Girl, what?" Tremaine leaned back, visibly stunned. "Why would he lie about something like that? And you're in a noncommitted relationship...why lie?"

"That's what I'm trying to figure out," Joanie said. "It's not like I asked for all his personal details, but the inconsistency is a huge red flag for me. Why not just be upfront?"

"Well," Dana interjected, "at least you caught it early. Better to know now than later. We ladies try to dismiss red flags, but don't, Joanie. Trust your gut."

"True," I said, "but it makes me question everything else. If he lied about that, what else is he hiding?"

Tremaine sighed dramatically, drawing our attention. "Speaking of men acting strange, Malik showed up at my house unannounced."

"No!" Dana gasped. "What happened?"

She leaned forward, her voice dropping to a conspiratorial whisper. "Yes, it was weird. He brought me my favorite Starbucks drink, trying to butter me up after a few nights ago. Said he was 'checking in.' But I could tell something was off. I told him outright he was acting jealous. You know what he said?"

"What?" Dana and I asked in unison.

"Nothing!" Tremaine exclaimed, throwing up her hands. "I think he was totally caught off-guard. He backpedaled so hard it was embarrassing. But the way he was acting...I don't know. Either his ego is bruised, or he's catching feelings. And neither of those is what I signed up for."

I chuckled. "A man child jealous...Tremaine, you really know how to pick them."

"Don't I, though?" she said with a wry grin. "But seriously, it's like they always want more than what we agreed on."

Dana shook her head. "You need to set some boundaries with him, Tremaine. If he's acting out that way, it's only going to get worse."

Tremaine raised her glass in a mock toast. "To boundaries."

"To boundaries," we echoed, clinking our glasses.

"Alright, Dana," Tremaine said, turning to her. "What about you? What's going on with Trey? Did you have a conversation with him yet?"

Dana sighed. She looked like the weight of her situation had settled heavily on her shoulders. "Yes, we talked, and he finally told me what's been going on. Come to find out, it's medical. He has some prostate issues, and that's what causing his...well, you know, the ED complications."

Dana said *ED* like spelling it out made it less awkward—like somehow *erectile dysfunction* was easier to swallow in acronym form. Truth was, nobody really talked about it, even though it was more common than folks liked to admit—especially with prostate issues involved. Still, knowing that didn't make saying it any less uncomfortable. Some things just landed heavy, no matter how delicately you tried to phrase them.

Tremaine and I nodded, our expressions softening.

"He didn't tell me for months," Dana continued. "Said he didn't want me to see him differently. But now that he's opened up, I can't help but wonder what else hasn't he told me. If he held back on something this important, what else could he be hiding?"

I reached over and squeezed my friend's hand. "Yeah, girl, I hate to say it, but Dana, you've been through so much together, you would think Trey would know he can trust you enough to tell you something as serious as that. I believe Trey loves you. At least he did open up to you. I think you have to give him some credit for taking the time to process this himself before opening up about this. It's a step in the right direction. Give him the benefit of the doubt."

"She's right," Tremaine added. "Men and vulnerability don't mix. It's hard for them to admit when they're struggling, especially with something that hits their manhood and their pride."

"I know," Dana said, nodding. "But after everything we've been through, I just wish he'd trusted me sooner."

"Maybe this is the beginning of a new level of trust," I offered. "He's always been your rock. Now it's time for him to lean on you."

"Maybe," Dana murmured, swirling her drink. Deep down, the questions lingered, unanswered and unsettling.

Our conversation shifted to lighter topics. I couldn't help but feel a knot of unease tightening in my stomach. Trust, vulnerability, boundaries—it seemed like all of us were navigating uncharted waters. And as I glanced at my two best friends, I realized that none of us had all the answers.

As we parted ways that evening, a single thought stayed with me: *What happens when the cracks we've ignored for so long finally split wide open?*

On the drive home, I replayed the conversations in my head. The red flag with Robert gnawed at me, a persistent itch I couldn't scratch away. Why lie about something as simple as family? And why do some men insist on making relationships more complicated than they need to be? My fingers hovered over my phone, tempted to send him a message and confront him right then and there, but I stopped myself. No. This needed to be addressed in person. I resolved to bring it up on our next date, no matter how awkward it might feel.

As I slowed to a stop at a red light, my phone buzzed on the passenger seat. I glanced down to see a message from James: *When can I see you again?*

A chill ran down my spine. The attention from two men should have felt flattering, but instead, it unsettled me. Two different paths, two potential pitfalls. Damn. What was I really getting myself into?

Chapter 19

Tremaine: A Quiet Chaos

Back at home, I poured myself another glass of wine and collapsed onto the couch. I inhaled deeply, exhaling as I took in my surroundings, almost as if seeing my space for the first time. My private domain—my happy place, as I liked to call it—was anything but orderly tonight. The faux-fur blanket I'd curled under while binge-watching Netflix a few nights ago was still balled up next to me. The coffee table was cluttered: an empty box of graham crackers, a saucer with the remnants of what could barely pass as a charcuterie board—sliced summer sausage, gouda cubes, and shriveled grapes. My laptop was perched on a stack of African-American literary classics, and a mug with cold ginger tea rested precariously on the edge of the table.

This wasn't me. At least, it wasn't the polished version of me that my friends saw—the Tremaine with her sharp wit, confident presence, and seemingly perfect façade. Tonight, though, my mind was as cluttered as the room. I needed order. Or maybe I just needed something—or someone—to fill the quiet. I continue to wrestle with my thoughts back to my last convo with my damn sister.

"Hell, maybe I should go to church with that heffa," I muttered to myself, chuckling dryly. "Maybe I do need Jesus."

The thought made me pause. Once upon a time, church wasn't just an afterthought; it had been my whole world. I used to be the choir director and a member of the praise team. Those were the days when my Sundays were filled with hymns and hallelujahs, and my weekdays were spent in choir rehearsals or organizing church fundraisers. So much of my childhood revolved around the church—my mother made sure of that.

Mama had dragged me and my four siblings to every service, every revival, every potluck. If the doors of the church were open, we were there. Our father? He never came. He was a good provider, but church wasn't his thing. It was Mama's realm, and she ruled it with the fervor of a true believer. She insisted that we be reared in the faith, though I always suspected it was less about religion and more about keeping us out of trouble.

I'd vowed early on that when I got "grown," I wasn't going to live my life shackled by the same routines. I wasn't about to miss out on life, as I believed my mother had. For all her devotion, Mama never seemed happy. It was as though she'd given everything to the church and left nothing for herself.

Is that why I've strayed so far away from it all? I wondered, taking a sip of wine.

Maybe my sister was right. Maybe I should be ashamed. Or maybe she was just projecting her own insecurities, her own guilt for staying in a marriage that was more prison than partnership. That thought gave me a flicker of satisfaction.

But as much as I tried to brush off her words, they lingered. *"A woman of your age, carrying on with a man young enough to be your son? Where's your dignity?"*

Where was my dignity? Was I living my life on my terms, or was I just running from something—trying to fill a void I didn't fully understand?

Malik hadn't texted since his unannounced visit, and the silence was louder than words. A part of me felt relieved. He'd crossed a line. But another part of me—a part I didn't want to admit existed—missed his attention. Or maybe it wasn't about him at all. Maybe I just missed attention, period. Malik. Max. Anyone.

My phone vibrated on the coffee table, pulling me from my thoughts. My heart leaped, hoping it was Malik, only to see an unknown number. I hesitated, the wineglass halfway to my lips, before opening the message.

I see you, Professor. Don't forget who you belong to.

The words sent a chill through me. I stared at the screen, the message feeling invasive, almost threatening. Was it Malik? Max? Someone else entirely?

I set the phone down, my hands trembling slightly. For all my independence, for all my rules about keeping things casual, was I losing control of the narrative? Of my own life? The room suddenly felt too small, the silence too oppressive.

Chapter 20

Dana: Gratitude in Sisterhood

As I folded the last of the laundry and set it aside, my thoughts drifted back to our meet-up earlier that evening. The laughter, the candid conversation, the unwavering support—I didn't know what I'd do without Joanie and Tremaine. They were my constants, my sounding boards, the anchors that kept me steady when life threw curveballs.

I was relieved to have them, grateful that I could lean on them during times like these. But even with that gratitude came a reluctance to share everything. Like the text I'd seen on Trey's phone earlier this week. The cryptic message from an unknown number—*Let's meet soon. I'm here when you need me*—still lingered in my mind. It had unsettled me, but I wasn't ready to tell Joanie and Tremaine. I knew exactly what I'd get: a flood of *oh hell nos* and *girl, you need to get to the bottom of this right now.*

Not yet. I needed more information first.

As I smoothed the duvet on the bed, I paused, letting my mind wander back to the beginning—when Trey and I first met. I'd been through a string of bad relationships in high school and my early twenties. The kind of relationships that left me questioning myself, my worth, and my ability to ever be truly loved. But Trey had changed all that.

When we first met, it was like he saw me—the real me. We'd talk for hours on the phone, sometimes until the sun came up. He was calm and measured, the perfect balance to my fiery temperament. Where I was quick to react, Trey was deliberate. Where I had a tendency to storm through situations, he had a way of anchoring me, making me feel safe in a way I hadn't experienced before.

Trey treated me like no one else ever had. It was never about grand gestures, though he'd surprised me with those occasionally. It was the little things—the way he'd listen, the way he made me feel like I was the only person in the room when he was around. With him, I felt seen, cherished, and whole.

Which is why this situation now—his secrecy about the prostate cancer and the text—rocked me to my core. Trey had always been my constant, my rock. We'd had struggles early on, sure, but we'd always been able to work through them together. I hated the idea of sounding boastful, especially with Joanie and Tremaine going through so much with the men in their lives, but the truth was, my marriage with Trey *was* different. It wasn't perfect, but it was strong—or at least it had been.

My mother's words echoed in my mind: *"Don't ever let your friendships dictate how you treat your marriage. Just because you're the only one with a man doesn't mean you have to shrink yourself to fit in. Show up for him, be present, and don't apologize for it."*

That advice had shaped how I approached my relationship with Trey. But now? Now, I didn't know what to think. The fear of losing him—not just physically, but emotionally—was like a shadow I couldn't escape. I tried to keep my faith, to tell myself that this was just a bump in the road, but deep down, I couldn't shake the unease. If something happened to Trey, if this medical condition became something more, what would I do?

Hearing the stories from Joanie and Tremaine—about the games men play, the lies, the red flags—only made it feel more unfair. Why would fate, God, or whatever force was out there bring this into our lives? What kind of cruel joke was this?

Just then, the sound of the footsteps down the hallway to our bedroom snapped me out of my thoughts. Moments later, Trey stepped into the room, his tie loosened and his shoulders slumped with exhaustion. He managed a tired smile as he sat on the bench at the foot of the bed.

"You're still up?" he asked, his voice soft.

"Barely," I replied, sitting up straighter. "Long day?"

He nodded, running a hand through his hair. "Yeah. But I'm glad I'm home."

I hesitated for a moment, my heart pounding. This was the moment. I had to bring it up. "Trey, there's something I need to ask you."

He looked up, his expression shifting to concern. "What is it?"

"Earlier this week, I saw a text on your phone," I said carefully, "from an unknown number. It said, *'Let's meet soon. It'll be worth your while.'*"

Trey froze, his face unreadable. For a moment, I braced myself for the worst, but then he sighed, reaching for his phone on the nightstand.

"That was from Derek," he said, unlocking the screen and pulling up the message. "He's a colleague. We were talking at work, and I guess I must've mentioned how hard all of this has been lately. He gave me the name of a therapist he thinks might help me mentally deal with everything going on."

Relief washed over me, but it was tempered by a pang of guilt. "A therapist?"

Trey nodded. "Yeah. I didn't want to overburden you. I've been trying to carry this on my own, but I'm realizing now that I can't. I need to be okay for both of us."

I reached out and placed a hand on his. "Trey, I told you, you don't have to go through this alone. I'm here. Whatever it takes, we'll get through this together."

He gave me a small, grateful smile, squeezing my hand. "Thanks babe. I don't know what I'd do without you."

As we lay down together, the weight on my chest began to lift. For the first time in weeks, I felt a sliver of hope. But deep down, I knew this was just the beginning. There was still a long road ahead, and I was determined to walk it with him every step of the way.

Chapter 21

Joanie: Complicated Dealbreakers

I adjusted my scarf as I stepped into the quaint coffee shop, the scent of freshly brewed espresso wrapping around me like a warm embrace. Robert was already seated at a table by the window, a book resting open in front of him. When he looked up and saw me, his face lit up with a smile that could melt away any lingering doubts—or at least that's what I wanted to believe.

"Joanie," he said, standing to pull out my chair. "You look lovely as always."

"Thank you," I replied, settling into the seat. "And you're still a gentleman. I appreciate that."

As we exchanged pleasantries, I found myself studying him more closely than usual. There was something so disarming about Robert's easy demeanor, but the questions swirling in my mind wouldn't let me relax completely. I decided to tread carefully.

"Robert," I began, swirling my latte with a tiny spoon, "I've been meaning to ask you something. It's probably nothing, but it's been on my mind."

"Of course," he said, setting his cup down and giving me his full attention. "What's on your mind?"

"You mentioned once that you have a son," I said, keeping my tone light, "but in another conversation, you said 'my sons.' It just caught me off guard. Do you have more than one?"

Robert's expression flickered, just for a second, before he smiled. "Ah, yes. I can see how that might seem confusing. I do have two sons, actually. I suppose I don't always mention both because...well, it's a complicated story."

I nodded, forcing a smile while my thoughts raced. Why hadn't he been upfront about this earlier? If it's so complicated, wouldn't that be more reason to explain it? Still, I decided to let it rest—for now.

As our conversation drifted back to lighter topics, I couldn't shake the feeling that Robert wasn't being entirely transparent. Grand gestures like his offer to take me to the Kinsey exhibit in Houston were wonderful, but they didn't erase the nagging red flags. And honestly, I couldn't help but wonder if Robert had a hidden agenda. Was he trying too hard to impress me?

I mean, the Kinsey showing definitely aligned with both of our personalities; that much was clear. But before I let him know my availability, I needed to set some things straight. There couldn't be any expectations or pressure. This wasn't going to be some grand romantic getaway unless I decided it was.

Then, another thought crept in: Was this about control? Did he need to make all the decisions to steer the relationship in his direction? It was probably an overreaction, but I couldn't ignore the possibility. I decided that if I agreed to this trip, I would make sure my girls were tracking me in the Life360 app, and I'd have my own transportation if needed.

Robert seemed authentic, but you just never know. This time, I wasn't going to ignore the small details or dismiss my gut feelings.

Later that evening, I paced the living room with my phone pressed to my ear, my stocking feet sinking into the plush carpet. Tremaine's familiar voice crackled through the line as I unloaded the details of my day.

"Tremaine, I don't know," I said, frustration lacing my voice. "Robert's great, but I feel like there's always something just beneath the surface. I want to trust him, but I'm seeing these small inconsistencies."

"Red flags?" Tremaine quipped, and I could hear the sound of a wine bottle uncorking in the background. "Join the club, sis. At least you're catching them now. I've got Malik showing up unannounced and acting like we're exclusive. And don't even get me started on Max."

I chuckled despite myself. "What about Max? Has he popped back up?"

"Not yet," she admitted, "but it's only a matter of time. Men like him never disappear for long. Malik, on the other hand, seems determined to keep me guessing. He's got this whole cool and confident thing going, but the moment I set boundaries, he acts out."

"So, what are you going to do?" I asked.

"Same thing I always do," Tremaine said with a wry laugh. "Keep them both at arm's length until one of them gives me a reason to cut them off entirely. But enough about my chaos. What about James? How's he measuring up?"

"James is..." I hesitated. "James is wonderful, honestly. But that's what makes me nervous. He's almost too perfect, you know? Like, what's the catch?"

"Girl, you're overthinking it," Tremaine said. "Just enjoy the attention. You're not beholden to either of them. Keep your options open."

I sighed, sinking deeper onto the couch as I curled by feet under me. "That's what I'm trying to do. But sometimes, I wonder if I'm just setting myself up for disappointment. These grand dates and big gestures are great, but what happens when the newness wears off?"

"Then you'll know who's worth keeping around," Tremaine said simply. "It's a process, Joanie. None of us have all the answers."

Tremaine's words hung in the air as I nodded. "You're right. It's just...exhausting sometimes."

I could hear Tremaine as she paused again to sip her wine "I get it, Joanie. It's a lot. And honestly, I see why some women stay in bad situations for so long. It's too damn cumbersome getting to know someone new, learning their quirks, their baggage, all of it."

I nodded, laughing softly. "You're so right. What a trip! I mean, here we are trying to sort out red flags like detectives, while Dana sits pretty with Trey. She doesn't have these relationship woes."

Tremaine raised an eyebrow. "True, but don't think for a second that marriage doesn't come with its own set of issues. Dana's got her battles, trust me. Trey may not be juggling women, but she's still navigating some heavy stuff with him right now."

I leaned back, thoughtful. "You're right. I guess the grass isn't greener on either side. We're all just trying to figure it out."

"Exactly," Tremaine said in agreement. "So, stop worrying about catching every single red flag. Just enjoy the moment while keeping your eyes open. You'll know when it's time to make a decision."

Now I paced the living room, Tremaine's words echoing in my head, but my thoughts kept pulling me inward. I sat down again and stared at my glass of wine, the liquid swirling slowly as if it held answers I couldn't find on my own. Could Tremaine be right? Was I overthinking everything? But the more I reflected, the more I started to see something uncomfortable.

"Maybe I'm the problem," I said aloud, the thought hanging heavy in the air. "Maybe I'm the one who needs to get clear about what I want."

For so long, I'd blamed the men in my life—Jackson's evasiveness, Robert's red flags, and James' elaborate outings. But was it fair to put it all on them? Had I set clear boundaries, or had I let my insecurities allow their behavior to slide? All the talk about accountability for men made me wonder: *Am I avoiding accountability for myself?*

I sighed and leaned back on the couch, the plush cushion doing little to ease the weight pressing on my chest. "I need to come clean with myself," I muttered, shaking my head. "It's time I set and maintain boundaries—not just to protect my emotional energy but to align with what I want out of a relationship. And one way to start is by practicing open, early communication. No more beating around the bush. I need to know right away if our values align, and if they don't, I need to walk away."

Maybe then, I'd recognize the deal breakers early and avoid settling—avoid repeating the same mistakes.

"I'm just not used to all this shit," I'd told Tremaine earlier, and now the words rang truer than ever.

"Welcome to dating in the modern age," Tremaine had said with a chuckle. "Now, pour yourself a glass of wine and relax. You've got this."

This time I took a gulp of my wine, thinking of her advice. It was a process, but one I wasn't sure I was fully ready for. Still, I resolved to keep moving forward, one step—and one boundary—at a time.

Chapter 22

Malik: Torn Loyalties

S itting on the edge of the bed, I watched Veronica move about the room with her usual air of confidence. She had that kind of beauty that could stop a man in his tracks—timeless, poised, effortless. I'd known from the moment we met that she wasn't the type to play by traditional rules. That's what drew me to her in the first place. When she suggested we explore a polyamorous relationship, it seemed like the perfect setup—honesty, open communication, clear boundaries. At least, that was the plan.

But lately, things hadn't felt so clear.

I leaned back, staring at the ceiling as she hummed to herself, prepping for her next playdate. That's what she called them. Veronica had no problem scheduling time for her "friends." And I'd always been fine with it—until Tremaine.

Tremaine. Her name alone sent a shiver through me. She was unlike anyone I'd ever met. Her charm, her maturity, her feistiness—it was intoxicating. With her, I felt something I hadn't felt in years. She didn't play games or hide behind pretense. Tremaine was real, and that terrified me.

"Malik, are you even listening to me?" Veronica's voice pulled me back to reality.

"Sorry, babe," I said, shaking my head. "What were you saying?"

She rolled her eyes, her tone playful but sharp. "I said, are you sure you're okay? You've been distracted lately."

"I'm fine," I lied, forcing a smile. "Just a lot on my mind."

She gave me a knowing look but didn't press further. That was Veronica—she respected boundaries, even when she suspected something was off. But this time, I knew I was the one crossing a line.

I hadn't told her about Tremaine. Not really. Veronica thought she knew everything, but I hadn't shared how deep my feelings were. Tremaine wasn't just another playdate. She made me question everything I thought I wanted. When I was with her, there were no rules, no age restrictions, no limits. I didn't feel like a man playing the field—I felt like a man, period. Mature, grounded, seen.

And that scared the hell out of me.

Later, as Veronica got ready to leave, I sat at the kitchen table scrolling aimlessly through my phone. I couldn't stop thinking about the last time I'd seen Tremaine—the way she had confronted me, her sharp wit cutting through my defenses like a knife.

"Malik, what are you doing here,?" she had asked, her voice laced with irritation. "You didn't call. Don't tell me you're catching feelings. We're not exclusive, remember?"

I hadn't known what to say. She'd caught me off guard, and I hated how vulnerable I felt in that moment. I wanted to tell her everything—that I couldn't stop thinking about her, that I wanted more. But the words wouldn't come. Instead, I'd stumbled through some half-baked excuse, making myself look like a fool.

Now, sitting here alone, I knew I couldn't keep this up. Veronica might think she had the upper hand in our arrangement, but the truth was, I wasn't playing by the rules anymore. This wasn't fun and games for me. Tremaine had changed everything.

I glanced at my phone, debating whether to text her. My heart pounded as I typed, erased, and retyped the same message. Finally, I settled on something simple: *Tremaine, we need to talk.*

Before I could hit send, Veronica walked in, her heels clicking against the hardwood floor. "I'm heading out," she said, leaning down to kiss my lips. "Don't wait up."

I nodded, my phone still in hand. "Have fun," I said, my voice hollow.

I paused for a second, hearing the door close behind her. I stared at the message on my screen. My finger hovered over the send button. Tremaine deserved honesty—real honesty, not the half-truths and excuses I'd been giving her—but was I ready to face the consequences?

I sighed, setting the phone down. The truth was, I didn't know if I was ready for anything anymore.

As I sat there in the silence, the weight of my choices pressing down on me, my phone buzzed with a new message. It was from Tremaine: *If you want to talk, you'd better come correct. I'm not in the mood for games.*

I stared at the screen, my heart pounding. Was I ready to come correct, or was I about to lose her for good?

Chapter 23

Max: Reflections

The faint sound of R & B singer Eric Roberson spilled softly from the speakers in the corner of my living room, setting a relaxed tone as I straightened the collar of my shirt. Tonight was another date night, but my mind wasn't fully present. My upcoming guest, Sherri, was sweet and accommodating—the kind of woman who didn't ask too many questions. It was easy with her, but lately, even the simplest encounters felt complicated.

As I poured myself a glass of Kentucky bourbon, my thoughts drifted back to Tremaine. Our last encounter had been...unexpected. When she flat out said she knew I was seeing other women, it caught me off guard. Not because it wasn't true—I'd never pretended otherwise—but because of the way she said it. There was no accusation in her tone, no bitterness, just...knowledge. She knew who I was and what I did, but something about her reaction that night unsettled me.

We'd always had an unspoken understanding. Tremaine knew how to read between the lines, and I'd thought I'd given her enough to tide her over until next time. But I'll admit, I'm not ready for a commitment—at least, I didn't think I was. Yet, I want Tremaine. She turns me on. She shook me when she revealed she was seeing someone else. I wasn't ready for that, which is why I used my physical resources to remind her of what she and I have and the great chemistry we make together. But after that incident at Joanie's gallery—and our last private conversation—it was clear something had shifted. She was asking questions I didn't have answers to, and for the first time, I felt like I'd underestimated her.

I swirled the amber liquid in my glass, staring into the depths as if it held some kind of revelation. "She's different," I muttered to myself. Different in ways that made me second-guess everything. Her charm, her maturity, her sharp wit—it all got under my skin in a way I hadn't anticipated. I'd always been able to compartmentalize my relationships, keep things casual and detached, but Tremaine made that difficult.

I sighed, setting the glass down and leaning against the counter. Maybe I'd pushed too far. Maybe I'd let her get closer than I should have. But it wasn't just her. Lately, I'd been feeling...restless. All the juggling, all the play, had started to lose its appeal. I wasn't sure if it was age catching up with me or if Tremaine had simply shifted my perspective. She'd opened my eyes to something I hadn't allowed myself to consider before: the possibility of more.

The sound of my phone vibrating on the counter snapped me out of my thoughts. I glanced at the screen—a text from Sherri confirming she'd be here in twenty minutes. Perfectly on time, as always. I knew how the evening would go: dinner, drinks, and then back here. It was predictable, comfortable, and yet uninspiring.

My mind wandered again to Tremaine—the way she carried herself, the fire in her eyes when she challenged me, the way she could make me feel like a boy out of his depth and a man in full control all at once. Even when she pretended not to care, I could sense it. There was more between us than she let on. Or maybe I was just projecting my own feelings onto her. Either way, it was dangerous territory.

I took another sip of bourbon, the burn grounding me. "I'll give her some time," I told myself. "Let her cool off. Then we'll see where we stand."

But even as I said it, I knew I was lying to myself. Time wasn't what I needed. What I needed was clarity. And if I didn't figure it out soon, I risked losing Tremaine for good.

Just then, the doorbell rang, pulling me back to the present. I straightened my shirt one last time and downed the rest of my drink. Whatever this evening held, I'd have to put my thoughts about Tremaine on hold. For now.

As I pulled open the door, a familiar smile greeted me, but instead of the usual anticipation, a sharp pang of realization hit me. Something felt off.

Sherri was as beautiful as any ray of sunshine and one of the three women I'd been seeing—not only was she drop dead gorgeous, she was intelligent, charming, always effortless company. Then there was Tremaine who had her own undeniable allure. And Monica, the one I'd spent time with last week. So far, I'd managed to juggle the three seamlessly, balancing my time and attention with the kind of precision only a true gentleman could master. I made sure each woman felt special when she was with me, attentive to her needs, present in the moment.

But tonight?

For the first time in years, I wasn't looking forward to what lay ahead, and that unsettled me more than I cared to admit.

Chapter 24

Dana: Holding It Together

The early-morning light filtered through my blinds as I laced up my sneakers, preparing for my usual gym session. I needed this—the physical release, the structure, the illusion of control. But no amount of weightlifting or treadmill runs could change the reality I was living in.

My life had shifted.

Trey's diagnosis had altered everything—our routine, our intimacy, our sense of normalcy. I had always envisioned us growing old together, but I never pictured navigating doctors' appointments, treatments, and specialist visits so soon. I knew Trey was trying, that he was leaning on me, trusting me to stand by him, but something in my gut told me he was still holding something back.

I replayed the moment I saw that text message from his friend—the one suggesting therapy. At first, I had been relieved when Trey explained it, but now, I wasn't so sure. What exactly had they talked about? Was there more he hadn't told me?

As I grabbed my gym bag and headed out the door, I scrolled through my phone contacts, hesitating for only a second before pressing Joanie's name.

She answered on the second ring. "Well, well, well, if it isn't the woman of mystery," she teased. "I was just about to text you. What's up?"

I sighed, unlocking my car and sliding into the driver's seat. "Nothing. Everything. I don't know."

"That bad?" she asked, her voice softening.

I stared at the dashboard, gripping the steering wheel. "I just...I'm trying, Joanie. I really am. But it's a lot. Taking care of Trey, managing his treatments, making sure he's okay emotionally as well as physically...and now, I'm second-guessing everything—wondering if there's more to this therapy suggestion than he let on."

Joanie paused. "You think he's still holding something back?"

I let out a dry chuckle. "At this point, I don't know what to think, but I can't shake this feeling."

"Dana, you've been married to this man for how long? Fifteen years? If your gut is telling you something, don't ignore it. But also, don't drive yourself crazy jumping to conclusions."

I exhaled. "Easier said than done."

Joanie clicked her tongue. "Look, I think you're overthinking this. Trey adores you, that's never been a question. And you know men, they hold things in because they think they're protecting us."

"That's just it," I said, rubbing my temple. "If he thinks hiding things from me is protecting me, what else is he keeping to himself?"

Joanie sighed. "I get it, I do. But maybe you're borrowing trouble. I think you need a distraction."

I smirked despite myself. "Oh yeah? You got something in mind?"

"As a matter of fact, yes. I'm hosting a private paint-and-sip night at the gallery. Just me, you, and Tremaine. I already have a chef lined up to serve some gourmet soul food, and I hired a jazz musician to set the mood. It's time we had some fun, just us girls."

I let my head fall back against the headrest, smiling for what felt like the first time all morning. "That actually sounds...amazing."

"Good, because you don't have a choice," Joanie said with a laugh. "I'll text you the details. And Dana?"

"Yeah?"

"Everything is going to be okay. Trey loves you, and you two will get through this. Just take it one day at a time."

I swallowed the lump in my throat. "Thanks, Joanie. I needed that."

"Anytime, sis. Now go lift some weights and work out all that stress."

I chuckled. "That's the plan."

As I ended the call, I stared out at the morning sky, inhaling deeply. Maybe Joanie was right. Maybe I *was* overthinking. But until I heard everything straight from Trey's mouth, I wasn't sure I'd be able to shake this feeling.

One way or another, I needed the whole truth.

Chapter 25

Joanie: Paint and Sip

The room was steeped in warmth, the air thick with the comforting scent of butter, brown sugar, and everything slow cooked with soul. Sweet notes of cinnamon and vanilla floated in the air, weaving through the deeper aromas of fried catfish and chicken, mingling gently with the savory pull of smoked meat and collard greens.

It smelled like nostalgia—like my granny's kitchen on a Sunday back in the day when the whole house buzzed with the promise of full plates and fuller hearts.

As I stood in the gallery making the final adjustments to the tables, I paused for a moment to take it all in. Tonight was all about relaxation. I'd curated an intimate evening for myself, Dana, and Tremaine—a private paint-and-sip night in the gallery. The idea was to take Dana's mind off what she'd been dealing with and give us all a chance to catch up in style. And what better way to lift the spirit than with a little soul food—comfort food, but with a modern spin.

Soft jazz like Kim Waters, and a touch of R&B floated through the air. I knew the girlfriends would enjoy some old school jams as well as some of the music by the newer artists—Avery Sunshine, Kem, Ledisi, they were some of our favorites—setting the perfect backdrop. I'd even hired a local chef to create an upscale soul food menu who brought my vision to life. In addition to what my nostrils so generously picked up, the menu boasted an array of mini portions to sample and savor. There were cornbread muffins, collard greens with smoked turkey, turnip green egg rolls, fried catfish bites, shrimp and grits cups, mac and cheese cups, and those heavenly mini chicken and waffles. The desserts looked just as divine—individual apple pies and peach cobbler cups arranged in a tempting display. Or as my daughters would say, *"had me in a chokehold*!" The gallery's ambience mirrored my vision: dim lighting highlighting bold, colorful abstract paintings and rare South African sculptures. My sanctuary transformed into my girlfriends safe haven, and tonight it belonged to us.

After Dana and Tremaine arrived, the room became alive with their warmth and laughter. Tremaine strode in first, her silver locs tied back in a sleek bun, her vibrant teal blouse catching the light. Dana followed closely behind, looking radiant despite the weight she'd been carrying. Her mustard-yellow dress hugged her figure, and her smile, though reserved, hinted at the relief of being surrounded by friends.

"Ladies, welcome!" I greeted, waving them toward the high-top table I'd set up with paints, brushes, and blank canvases. "Tonight, we're going to create masterpieces and sip wine like queens."

"And eat like them too, I see," Tremaine teased, eyeing the spread. "Joanie, you really outdid yourself."

Dana's eyes softened as she hugged me. "Thank you, Joanie. This is exactly what I need."

As we settled in, the conversation flowed as freely as the wine. Dana started by catching us up on Trey.

"His prognosis is promising," she said, her voice steady but tinged with emotion. "The specialist is optimistic, and Trey's finally opening up more, but I'm still processing everything. It's a lot."

Tremaine reached across the table and squeezed Dana's hand. "You're handling it with grace, Dana. Don't forget to take care of yourself too."

"I'm trying," Dana admitted, her eyes glistening, "but sometimes I'm just so...tired. And honestly, seeing the two of you thrive in your...unconventional relationships, it's hard not to feel a little envious."

"Envious?" I asked, surprised. "Dana, you and Trey have something special. That kind of love isn't easy to come by."

She smiled wistfully. "I know. I love Trey deeply, but there are moments when I wonder what it would be like to have the freedom you two seem to have. Of course, it's just a fleeting thought. Trey is my soul mate, and I'd never trade what we have."

"Trust me," Tremaine interjected, swirling her wine, "the freedom isn't all it's cracked up to be. I haven't heard from Max lately, and Malik... Well, let's just say he's been acting strange—showing up uninvited, making snide remarks. Like the other day, he told me, it must not be my turn. Can you believe that?"

Dana and I exchanged glances.

Tremaine threw up her hands. "As in, my schedule is full, so his turn to see me hasn't come around yet. Like he's standing in line at the DMV for some damn affection from me. Boy, bye!"

Dana and I exchanged glances before bursting into laughter. "Oh, Tremaine," Dana said, shaking her head. "You always have the most interesting stories."

"Interesting is one way to put it," Tremaine muttered, rolling her eyes. "But enough about my mess. Joanie, what's the latest with your two suitors?"

"Oh, Lord." I groaned, taking a sip of wine. "James and Robert are practically competing for my time and attention. Morning texts, evening texts—it's like clockwork. And honestly, it's a bit much. But somehow, I've managed to text the right responses to the right person so far."

The room erupted in laughter. "Joanie, you're living the dream," Tremaine said with a wink.

"More like navigating a minefield," I replied. "It's fun, but it's extremely different from what I've been accustomed to. And let's not forget the red flags. Robert's got his inconsistencies, and

James...well, he's almost *too* perfect. Makes me wonder what's hiding under the surface."

Dana leaned forward, her tone serious. "Just be careful, Joanie. You deserve someone who's genuine."

"I know," I said, nodding. "That's why I'm taking my time. No rushing, no settling. Just trying to figure it all out."

The more wine I poured and refilled my girls glasses, the louder our laughter grew. Our brushstrokes got bolder, our paintings more abstract and the weight of our individual struggles seemed to lighten. By the time the night ended, I felt a renewed sense of gratitude for these women. They were my sisters, my confidantes, my anchors.

Tremaine and Dana had helped tidy up the gallery before they left but a few final touches remained. After they were gone, I moved through the quiet space, finishing the cleanup at my own pace. There was something peaceful about it—the stillness, the soft hum of the evening settled in. I had just wiped down the last table when my phone buzzed. It was a message from Robert. *I have a surprise planned for us. Hope you're free this weekend.* I stared at the screen, my heart fluttering and my mind racing. A surprise? What could that mean? And more importantly, was I ready for it?

Chapter 26

Dana: Facing the Future

Sitting in the specialist's office, I felt like the air had been sucked out of the room. The doctor's words replayed in my mind on an endless loop, but none of it seemed to fully register. Trey sat beside me, his hand resting on mine, his thumb tracing small circles over my skin—a gesture meant to comfort me, though I could tell he was the one who needed reassurance.

"The prognosis is good," the doctor had said, his tone measured but optimistic. "With treatment, we can manage this, and Trey should recover well. But it's going to take time, patience, and a commitment to the process."

Time. Patience. Commitment. They sounded simple enough, but in reality, they carried the weight of uncertainty—and change. I looked at Trey, his expression calm but distant, as if he was already grappling with what this would mean for us.

"Dana," he said softly, pulling me from my thoughts as we walked to the car, "you've been quiet. Talk to me."

I swallowed hard, trying to find the right words. "I'm just...processing everything. It's a lot, Trey. I'm scared, but I don't want to make this about me. I need to know how you're feeling."

He sighed, leaning back against the headrest as we sat in the car. "Honestly? I'm scared too. Not just about the treatment, but about us—about how this changes everything."

"It doesn't change us," I said firmly, reaching for his hand. "We're still us, Trey. This is just a detour, not the end of the road."

He looked at me then, his eyes glassy but steady. "I know. And I'm grateful for you, Dana. I've been selfish, trying to carry this alone, and that wasn't fair to you. But now...I think we need to have some real conversations—about everything."

I nodded, bracing myself for what was to come. "We do. And we need to talk about how we're going to share this with the boys and the rest of the family. They need to know, Trey. But we have to be strong when we tell them."

Trey nodded slowly. "You're right. We'll tell them together. But I need you to know something, Dana." He turned to face me fully, his expression raw and vulnerable. "I need you to know that no matter what happens, you are my anchor. You're the reason I've been able to get through even the toughest days. I'm sorry I didn't tell you sooner. I was scared of being weak in front of you."

I blinked back tears, squeezing his hand tightly. "Trey, you're not weak. You're human. And you don't have to face this alone. We're a team, remember? Always."

He smiled faintly, the tension in his shoulders easing slightly. "Always."

As we drove home, we started planning how to break the news to our sons. They were both in their twenties now, carving out their own paths in life, but this would undoubtedly be hard for them to hear. Trey insisted on taking the lead in the conversation, but I made it clear that we were doing this together.

We also talked about what this meant for us as a couple. The late-night dinners we'd grown accustomed to, the spontaneous road trips, the intimacy we'd always cherished—all of it might look different now. But as we navigated those uncertainties, one thing became clear: our love was steadfast. It had weathered storms before, and this would be no different.

When we finally pulled into the driveway, Trey reached over and took my hand again. "Thank you for sticking with me, babe. I don't say it enough, but I don't know what I'd do without you."

I smiled, leaning over to kiss his cheek. "You'll never have to find out."

Chapter 27

Joanie: A Purposeful Family Call

The familiar chime of FaceTime filled my quiet living room as I propped my phone on the coffee table, adjusting the angle to capture the best lighting. Within seconds, the faces of my two beautiful daughters popped up on the screen, their energy instantly lighting up my space.

"Good morning, ladies," I greeted, smiling warmly.

"Morning, Mom!" cheered Aisha, my youngest, her glowing face framed by the backdrop of her LA apartment. Her natural curls bounced as she adjusted her camera. "You look fabulous as usual. Spill it. Have you found us a new stepdad yet?"

Before I could answer, her older sister, Layla, who was calling from her New York apartment, jumped in. "Girl, please. You already know the answer to that. She needs to take a class or something first. Ms. Independent I-Don't-Need-A-Man is not about to be out here looking for some stepdad for us."

I rolled my eyes playfully, shaking my head. "Whatever, y'all. If only you knew how much excitement I've been having lately, you'd be surprised."

"Excitement? Spill the tea, Mom," Aisha teased, leaning closer to the screen.

"Oh, there's nothing to spill. And y'all need to learn how to stay out of grown folks' business. Anyway, we're not here to talk about me. Let's focus on the event," I said, redirecting the conversation to the reason for the call. Every year, the three of us hosted an annual event for high school senior girls pursuing college majors in the arts. It was a tradition that had grown close to our hearts.

"Fine," Layla conceded, smiling. "How's the sponsor list coming along?"

"It's looking fantastic," I replied. "We've added some new names to our usual heavy hitters. It's the largest sponsor list we've ever had."

"That's amazing," Aisha exclaimed. "But what about the guest speaker? Have you locked someone in?"

"Not yet," I admitted. "I have a couple people in mind, but I'm open to suggestions. Let's keep it fresh, a younger perspective is always good."

"What about getting someone from New York? I'm thinking an up-and-coming Black female artist." Layla suggested. "I know a couple of people who would know of someone who might be available. I'll make some calls."

"And I can reach out to a few of my contacts as a backup," Aisha added. "Maybe someone who can talk about breaking into the dancing arts as a woman of color."

"Perfect," I said, jotting down notes. "We also need to finalize the details for the silent auction. I'm thinking of donating one of the South African pieces from the gallery."

"*Oooh.* The one with the bold reds and golds?" Layla asked, her eyes lighting up. "That one would be perfect."

"Exactly," I said with a nod. "It'll draw some great bids, and the proceeds will help us increase the scholarship fund."

"Speaking of the scholarship fund," Aisha chimed in, "how many girls are we planning to support this year?"

"The goal is twenty-five," I replied. "We did twenty last year, and I'd love to expand it. These girls need all the encouragement and resources they can get."

"I'm so proud of us," Layla said, her voice softening. "It's amazing to see how far this scholarship fund event has come. I mean, who would've thought when we started this ten years ago that it would grow into something this big?"

"It's because of the passion you two have brought to it," I said, beaming with pride. "You both inspire me every day with your dedication to the arts. And it's because of that dedication that these young women have role models like you to look up to."

"Okay, Mom, you're going to make me cry," Aisha said, fanning her face dramatically.

"Same," Layla added with a laugh. "But seriously, Mom, you're the real MVP. None of this would exist without you."

"We're a team," I said firmly. "And together, we're going to make this year's event the best."

My girls continued to converse, affectionately asking about their aunties.

"How are Auntie Tremaine and Auntie Dana?" Aisha asked.

"Dana's doing okay," I said carefully. "She and Trey have been dealing with some challenges, but she's strong as always. And Tremaine...well, let's just say she's keeping life interesting.".

Layla laughed knowingly. "Auntie Tremaine is always up to something. That woman...I swear she could write her own novel."

"You have no idea," I said with a chuckle, leaving it at that. I knew better than to share too much of *Auntie Tremaine's* indiscretions. What Layla thought she knew was one thing—what I wasn't going to do was spill any tea on my bestie, at least not to my daughter. Some things are sacred. Somes stories are meant only for the ears of my tribe—a grown ass woman.

After the call ended and the laughter faded, I sat back and stared at my phone. The excitement about the event filled me with pride, but Aisha's playful question lingered in the back of my mind: Had I found them a new stepdad yet? If only they knew about James and Robert. If only they knew how close I was to making decisions that could shift everything. For now, though, I'd keep it all to myself.

Chapter 28

Tremaine: A Face-off

As I leaned back on my couch, wineglass in hand, I stared at the message I had sent Malik: *If you want to talk, you'd better come correct. I'm not in the mood for games.* It was bold and probably more confrontational than necessary, but I was tired of beating around the bush. Malik had pushed me to the edge with his possessive antics. If he couldn't handle the truth, then it was time to let him go.

My phone buzzed. For a moment, I hesitated, my finger hovering over the screen. What now? Malik was predictable, but this...this energy felt different.

"Oh, come on," I muttered to myself, finally unlocking the phone. The name that popped up wasn't Malik's. It was Max. *Great,* I thought sarcastically. *What could he possibly want?*

I opened his message, which read: *Tremaine, I know I've been distant, but we need to talk. Can we meet?*

I scoffed out loud. "Distant?" That was an understatement. Max's version of distant was weeks of radio silence followed by an overly charming reappearance that he assumed would erase his absence. But not this time.

"You're on thin ice," I muttered under my breath as I typed back: *What's there to talk about, Max? You've made it pretty clear where you stand—or should I say, where you don't stand?*

His response came quicker than I expected: *You might think you know the whole story, but you don't. Give me a chance to explain.*

I set the phone down and took a long sip of wine. Explaining was Max's favorite thing to promise, but he rarely delivered. Still, something about his tone made me pause. Was he about to confess something? And did I even want to hear it?

Before I could overthink it, the doorbell rang. My stomach flipped. "Don't tell me he's pulled another one of his dramatic pop-ups," I grumbled as I walked to the door.

But it wasn't Max. It was Malik, standing there with a bouquet of bright yellow sunflowers and an expression that hovered between sheepish and smug.

"What are you doing here?" I asked, folding my arms across my chest.

"I got your message," he said, holding up the flowers like a peace offering. "I wanted to...come correct."

I stared at him for a moment, torn between irritation and amusement. "You can come in, but you've got five minutes to explain yourself."

Malik followed me into the living room, his eyes darting around the space. "Your place is always cozy," he said, trying to break the tension.

"Don't try to charm me, Malik. Just get to the point," I said, setting the flowers on the coffee table.

He sighed, running a hand over his close-faded haircut. "Look, Tremaine, I know I've been...out of line. Showing up uninvited, acting jealous. It's not fair to you."

"You think?" I said, raising an eyebrow. "So what's your excuse?"

He hesitated, his gaze dropping to the floor. "I guess I...didn't realize how much I care about you until recently. And maybe I don't know how to handle that."

I blinked, caught off guard. "Care about me?" The words hung in the air, heavy with implication. "Malik, we agreed this wasn't about feelings. It was supposed to be casual."

"I know," he said quickly, "but you...you're different, Tremaine. You make me want more. I get that you're not looking for anything serious, but I can't pretend like this is nothing for me anymore."

His honesty hit me harder than I expected. But before I could respond, my phone buzzed again. Another message from Max: *I'm outside. We need to talk.*

I froze, my heart racing as I glanced at Malik who was still waiting for an answer. *What the hell is going on tonight?*

As I stood there, torn between two men and their sudden confessions, another notification from my phone shattered the tense silence. This time, I didn't even have to guess who it was. The question was, what the hell was I going to do about it?

Chapter 29

Joanie: A Tale of Two Men

I fiddled with my earrings out of habit to make sure they laid just right, smoothing the silk of my dress as I took one last glance in the mirror. Tonight was different. James had promised something spectacular, and though I tried to downplay my excitement, I couldn't deny the anticipation thrumming beneath my skin. After Robert's inconsistencies, I was craving something that felt effortless, smooth—a true connection without doubts creeping in at every turn.

James had texted earlier with nothing but the words: *Be ready at seven. Dress elegantly.* No hints, no details. Just intrigue.

When I stepped outside, a sleek black Town Car idled at the curb. James leaned casually against the door, dressed in a crisp navy suit that hugged his frame just right.

"You look stunning," he said, opening the door for me.

"I try," I teased, slipping inside. "So, are you finally going to tell me where we're going?"

He smirked. "Not yet. Just sit back and enjoy."

The city lights blurred past as we drove deeper into downtown Dallas. When we pulled up in front of an elegant high-rise, I turned to him with a questioning look.

"A hotel?" I arched a brow.

James chuckled. "Not quite. Come on."

James led me through a private elevator, the quiet hum of its ascent only adding to the anticipation curling in my chest. When the doors slid open, I stepped onto a rooftop terrace bathed in dim, golden light. The heart of Dallas stretched out before me, shimmering against the night, but what truly took my breath away was the jazz trio nestled in the corner of the terrace.

Perched atop the sleek high-rise, the trio—saxophone, upright bass, and jazz guitar—set the perfect mood, their smooth melodies floating effortlessly through the air. Plush seating and warm, ambient lighting gave the venue a chic yet intimate feel, the kind of place that felt exclusive but never pretentious. Around us, guests sipped craft cocktails, their hushed laughter mingling with the music and the gentle evening breeze.

Then, my eyes landed on the candlelit table set just for us. The flickering glow cast soft shadows across the crisp linen, making the polished silverware gleam. It was understated elegance, the kind of effortless romance you didn't have to announce—you just *felt* it.

The trio, dressed in sharp but easy-going attire, played a mix of classic jazz standards and modern improvisations, their melodies drifting over the edge of the rooftop. Beyond the terrace, the Trinity River stretched out beneath the vast Texas sky, the illuminated Reunion Tower standing proudly in the distance. The city below pulsed with life, yet up here, it felt like time had slowed.

I exhaled, barely realizing I'd been holding my breath.

"James," I murmured, my voice nearly lost in the music. "This is...beautiful."

"I know how much you appreciate the arts," he said, leading me to the table. "I wanted to give you an experience, not just a dinner."

I studied him carefully. The effort, the attention to detail—it was thoughtful. But it was also grand. Too grand? *Why are you trying so hard?* I wondered, forcing a smile watching the waiter pour our wine.

We settled into an easy conversation, the kind that flowed as naturally as the jazz surrounding us. He spoke about his travels, his appreciation for culture, and I found myself relaxing into the rhythm of his company. Yet, there was a nagging thought in the back of my mind. Something about James was always so perfectly curated.

"Tell me something real," I said, sipping my wine. "Not something polished. Something about you I wouldn't find in a well-rehearsed conversation."

James hesitated, then exhaled a quiet laugh. "Alright, you got me. I tend to orchestrate moments. It's a flaw of mine. I like to create an environment where everything feels right."

"And why is that?"

He toyed with the stem of his glass. "Control, I suppose. I don't like leaving things to chance."

I nodded slowly, taking in his words. *Control.* That was it. James was intoxicating, but was he too measured? Too practiced?

"And what happens when you can't control things?" I asked.

He smirked, eyes gleaming. "Then I adapt."

The answer satisfied me for now, but I tucked my questions away for later. For tonight, I let myself revel in the moment—the music, the atmosphere, and the undeniable chemistry between us. But somewhere in the back of my mind, a voice whispered: *Be careful, Joanie. Not all grand gestures are what they seem.*

The next evening, I found myself sitting across from Robert at our usual spot, a cozy café, the warmth of my latte doing little to ease the weight of our conversation. After last night's extravagant date with James, tonight felt more grounded—yet no less complicated. I had come here for answers, but as usual, life had its own agenda.

My phone vibrated. I stared at the screen, Jackson's name glowing like a ghost from the past. *Hey, beautiful. I miss you. Are you available? I would love to see you.*

My heart lurched—half in irritation, half in something I wasn't quite ready to name. Of all the people to pop up right now, it had to be him. The man who had fed me empty words and half-truths, the man who had taken up space in my life without ever fully claiming it. I had no one to blame but myself for unblocking him. Curiosity had overpowered my better judgment. As much as I pretended not to care, some part of me—maybe the loneliest part—needed to know if he'd try to reach out. If he missed me. If I still crossed his mind.

I exhaled sharply, rolling my eyes. *The audacity.*

Robert sat across from me, still looking like he was waiting for my verdict. But my mind had already checked out of our conversation. This text had thrown me off balance. I wasn't about to let Jackson slither back into my life with a lazy "I miss you." Not after the mess he left behind.

But still, I hesitated. Not to respond—but to decide whether this was worth my energy at all.

Robert noticed my distraction. "Everything okay?"

I quickly locked my phone and forced a smile. "Yeah. Just something I wasn't expecting."

Robert tilted his head slightly, studying me. "You sure? You seem distracted."

I waved a hand dismissively. "It's nothing. Anyway, I wanted to ask you something."

His expression eased, and he leaned forward slightly. "Ask away."

I leaned back in my chair, studying Robert over the rim of my latte. There was something about him—polished, charming—but still something felt slightly off. I decided to tread lightly.

"Tell me something about you that I don't already know," I said casually, tapping my fingers against the ceramic mug.

Robert chuckled. "Now that's an interesting question. What do you think you know?"

I smirked. "Well, I know you're an art lover, you enjoy a good jazz set, and you have a way with words, but what's something you wouldn't put on a dating profile?"

He took a slow sip of his coffee, a thoughtful look crossing his face. "I suppose I can be a bit of a perfectionist. I don't like loose ends."

I raised an eyebrow. "Loose ends like what?"

He exhaled, rubbing the back of his neck. "Like relationships that don't quite close properly. Friendships that fizzle out but never officially end. I don't like not knowing where I stand with people."

I nodded, letting his words settle between us. "So does that mean you always tell the full truth—no omissions?"

He hesitated for a second too long. "I try to."

There it was. That hesitation. That space where honesty should live, but instead, uncertainty crept in.

I stirred my latte slowly, watching the steam rise, my thoughts clouded just as much as the surface of my drink. I wasn't trying to go down this road again, but something about Robert still wasn't sitting right with me. I wasn't trying to nitpick, but I also wasn't about to ignore my gut.

I glanced up at him, keeping my tone light. "You know, I've been thinking a lot about our last conversation about past relationships."

Robert set his cup down and gave me a measured look. "Oh yeah? What about them?"

I shrugged, keeping my voice casual. "Just how people choose to reveal things over time. Sometimes, it's not about hiding anything, just about when they feel comfortable enough to share."

He nodded slowly. "That's fair. Some things don't come up right away. But that doesn't mean they're meant to be kept secret."

I studied his face, looking for any flicker of unease. "True. But sometimes I wonder—how do you know if you're getting the full picture? Or if someone is just curating what they want you to see."

Robert exhaled, tilting his head slightly. "Joanie, if you're asking if I'm holding anything back, you can just ask me directly."

I held his gaze, measuring my words. "I guess I just don't want to be in a situation where I find out things I should've known upfront."

He leaned back in his chair, crossing his arms slightly. "I get that. But Joanie, you know what I've told you so far. If there's something specific on your mind, tell me."

I offered a small smile, though the unease hadn't left me. "I'm just making conversation, Robert."

He nodded, but his eyes didn't quite meet mine. There was a flicker—just enough to make me pause. Like his face said everything his mouth refused to. And just like that, I knew: He was holding something back.

"Good. Because I don't want you looking at me like I'm hiding something."

I took a slow sip of my latte, deciding to let it rest—for now. But in the back of my mind, the nagging feeling didn't fade.

I offered him a small nod before heading out of the café. The moment I stepped onto the sidewalk, I unlocked my phone and reread Jackson's message.

I hovered over the keyboard. I could ignore him. I could block him. I could hit him with the same dismissiveness he had given me time and time again.

Or I could get the closure I never had.

My fingers hovered over the screen before finally typing, I'm free. Let's talk.

Chapter 30

Tremaine: When Two Worlds Collide

I paced my living room, gripping the stem of my wineglass a little too tightly. Yeah, I know—another glass of wine. But something about that first sip always took the edge off, even if only for a moment. The tension inside me coiled like a snake, tightening with every unanswered thought. Max's message had been brief but direct: *We need to talk. I'm outside.*

I exhaled sharply, setting my glass down with a little more force than necessary. The last thing I wanted was a confrontation, but something told me I wasn't going to get out of this evening without one.

Malik stood there, hands in his pockets, his signature smirk absent for once.

"Tremaine," he said, his voice unusually careful, "can we talk?"

I folded my arms. "That depends. Are you here to be honest or just to pacify me?"

His jaw tightened, and he stepped inside, brushing past me like he belonged there. I shut the door behind him, watching as he ran a hand over his head.

"Tremaine, I came here because I need to tell you something, and I feel like it needed to be said in person."

I raised an eyebrow, not sure if I should sit down for what he was about to say, "Go on."

Before he could speak, my phone buzzed on the table. My chest tightened, breath catching for half a second. I didn't have to look—I already knew who it was.

Damn it.

Malik frowned. "Expecting someone? "

Before I could answer, my phone buzzed again—and again. The sound cut through the silence like an alarm.

"Someone is blowing you up, girl," he added, glaring. "Oh, so you just gonna act like we don't hear all those notifications?"

I closed my eyes for a second, trying to breathe through the pressure building behind my temples.

"Malik, this is too much right now," I said, my voice tight. "Give me a minute."

I picked up my phone, already knowing who it was: Max. Of course it was Max.

No hesitation. No overthinking this time.

I typed: Max, tonight's not good. I'm asking you to leave now. I'll let you know when there's a better time.

I hit send before I could second-guess myself.

Intentionally, I ignored Malik's question, inhaling deeply before glancing down at my phone. Max responded like clockwork. His name flashed on the screen with another text message. My pulse quickened.

Max: *I need to see you. I've given you space, but you've been on my mind. Stop playing games, Tremaine. Tomorrow. I'll give you until tomorrow.*

I groaned inwardly. *Here we go.*

My phone buzzed again before I could respond, Max's name lighting up the screen. I hesitated, glancing at Malik, who had his arms crossed, watching me read the message.

Max's text read: *We need to talk. Let's not pretend this is nothing.*

I sighed, shaking my head: *Tomorrow. I will call you, Max.*

I hit send, and hopefully, this was my last send to Max for this evening.

Malik, unaware of the nature of the messages, looked at me quizzically, his dark eyes searching mine. "Tremaine, what exactly are we doing here? Because I can't keep doing this."

I met his gaze, my mind a chaotic mess. I had prided myself on being in control, on keeping things casual. But standing here, listening to Malik's sudden need for clarity while Max lingered in the background—figuratively and literally—it all felt like too much.

"Malik, you came here to talk, so talk."

He hesitated, running a hand over his beard as if deciding how much to say.

I was blindsided. Just as I was about to press him, his phone buzzed. He frowned and pulled it out.

"Give me a sec," he muttered, stepping back.

I crossed my arms, watching his face as he answered. His entire demeanor shifted.

"Veronica? What's wrong?"

I felt a little off—lightheaded, but not drunk. I knew better. Something was up. The mood turned on a dime. Again. I folded my arms, leveling my gaze at Malik. "Veronica?" I repeated, my voice laced with suspicion.

Malik sighed, sliding his phone back into his pocket. "Yeah. That's part of what I wanted to tell you about."

I narrowed my eyes. "Oh, so who's Veronica, and what about her?"

He exhaled, fiddling with his beard again. "Tremaine, Veronica is my wife. And before you go off, let me explain: When I got involved with Veronica, I thought the whole polyamory thing wouldn't be a problem. I thought it would be simple—no pressure, no expectations. It started out with the playdates just to add a little fun to our relationship."

I blinked. "Excuse me? Did you just say polyamory thing?"

Malik took a cautious step toward me. "I didn't expect to feel this way. I didn't expect to want more than what we have. And now, I know I don't want to be a part of that lifestyle anymore. I want to be with you. Just you."

I felt my stomach twist in a mix of shock and fury. "You wait until now to tell me this? And just like that, I'm supposed to be okay with you and Veronica, your playdates. What the hell?"

Before he could respond, my phone buzzed yet again. Max. Another text. Another disruption.

Malik's eyes flickered toward my phone as I turned the screen downward on the table, my frustration boiling over. "Do you need to deal with that, or should we finish this conversation?"

I barely had a moment to react before Malik's phone buzzed once more. His expression shifted, tension stiffening his posture.

"Damn. All these interruptions," he muttered, stepping back, putting his phone to his ear.

I crossed my arms, watching his face as he answered, still trying to process all of what I'd just heard. His entire demeanor shifted.

"Veronica? Calm down. Give me about an hour. I'll get there as soon as I can," he spoke into the phone as if I couldn't hear him.

My stomach twisted. Whatever it was, it wasn't small. And then, like a tsunami crashing without warning, the chaos hit—hard. Everything unraveled. Again.

I clenched my fists, trying to control the rage simmering beneath my skin. My voice dropped, low and cutting. "Did you just say *your wife*?"

The words hung in the air, thick and suffocating. And then, it hit me: Veronica.

Joanie had mentioned her before—the woman who had casually admitted to being in an open marriage, who had spoken so freely about giving her husband playdates with other women. That Veronica.

My stomach churned. "Wait a damn minute. Veronica?" I snapped, stepping closer. "As in Joanie's client Veronica? The woman who stood in her gallery and told her how she lets her husband have his fun?"

Malik exhaled, and by his actions, he clearly didn't know what else to do with his damn hands, there he stood like rewound toy, rubbing a hand over his beard again. "Tremaine, listen—"

"Oh, I'm listening," I shot back, my voice trembling with fury. "I'm just wondering if you've completely lost your damn mind. You mean to tell me that this entire time, you had a whole damn wife at home? That you brought your ass over here, into my home, into my bed while your wife was somewhere handing out damn hall passes?"

Malik sighed, his eyes widening. "I thought it wouldn't be a problem. Veronica and I agreed—"

"I don't give a damn what you and Veronica agreed to," I cut him off, my voice rising. "You put me in harm's way, Malik! You should've given me the choice to be a part of this instead of sneaking around like some low-down, lying—"

Before I could finish, Malik's phone buzzed. He pulled it out, glanced at the screen, and put up a finger.

A finger.

He actually had the nerve to silence me while he answered his damn phone.

I saw red.

"Oh, you did not just shush me," I seethed, every ounce of my restraint snapping in half.

"Veronica, calm down," he said into the phone, his voice suddenly soft, urgent. "Give me about an hour. I'll get there as soon as I can."

I scoffed, shaking my head, feeling the rage inside me begin to erupt like a volcano.

"You know what? Get out, Malik. Get the hell out of my house, out of my presence, out of my damn life. I don't have the mental capacity to deal with your bullshit right now. You have me twisted—twisted and mixed up with someone else."

Malik hesitated. "Tremaine, let me explain—"

"No! Get. Out. Now."

He exhaled, slipping his phone back in his pocket and nodding slowly. "Alright. I'll go."

He reached the door, then turned around like he suddenly remembered his lines. That same dumb deer-in-the-headlights expression was plastered across his face. "I didn't want it to be like this," he said, as if that changed anything.

I stared at him, my body shaking with rage, but I said nothing. I had nothing left to say.

Chapter 31

Joanie: An Unforgettable Evening

I stared at my reflection in the mirror, adjusting the delicate gold earrings that dangled just above my shoulders. My thoughts swirled as I applied the final touch of lipstick, trying to shake the uneasy feeling that had settled in my chest. Dating had become more of a strategic game than an organic experience. I had promised myself that I'd take things slow, but with James, the pace felt set at his speed, and I wasn't sure how I felt about that.

After the extravagant helicopter ride, I couldn't imagine what else he had up his sleeve tonight. I liked James, there was no denying that. He was confident, charming, and well-connected. But he was also meticulous, orchestrating every moment with an almost calculated precision. I wondered if it was just his way, or if I was walking into something I couldn't quite name yet.

My phone buzzed. A message from James: *I'll be downstairs in five. Hope you're ready for an unforgettable evening.*

I exhaled, picking up my clutch and headed out.

The drive through downtown Dallas was smooth, and James, as always, was effortlessly engaging. We pulled up to a lavish high-rise, the kind that oozed exclusivity. The doorman greeted James like an old friend, and within moments, we were escorted to the penthouse suite.

The moment we stepped in, I was engulfed in the ambience—dim lighting, soft candlelight flickering against polished marble, and the smooth sound of a saxophone setting the mood. A select crowd of well-dressed art lovers and influencers mingled with glasses of wine in hand. My eyes widened as I took in the stage setup—intimate, elegant, and centered around none other than my favorite singer Eric Roberson.

I turned to James, unable to hide my shock. "You've got to be kidding me."

He smirked. "You mentioned he was one of your favorites. Thought you'd enjoy something special."

I could only shake my head in disbelief. This wasn't just a date; this was an experience, curated with precision. The warmth of Eric's voice filled the room as he performed, his smooth tones carrying through the penthouse, pulling me deeper into the moment.

James leaned in, his voice just above a whisper. "You're enjoying yourself, I hope."

I turned to him, studying his expression. He was pleased with himself, but not arrogant. He was attentive, present, and for once, I allowed myself to just be in the moment.

"I am," I admitted, "but you're really raising the bar here."

James chuckled. "Good. I'd hate for you to settle for anything less."

We talked over drinks, our conversation flowing effortlessly. Music, art, travel—the topics danced between us like a well-rehearsed melody. I found myself captivated but still cautious. As much as I enjoyed the evening, I reminded myself of the promise I had made—to take things slow, to ensure that this was real before letting my guard down.

Like clockwork, James gentlemanly led me to the passenger side of his car, opening the door with his usual charm. The ride back was quiet but comfortable, filled with the soft hum of jazz playing through the speakers. When we reached my place, he put the car in park and turned toward me with an easy smile. He didn't push, didn't suggest more than a lingering gaze and a warm good night. No pressure. No expectation. Just the subtle electricity of an unspoken moment lingering between us. I exhaled, grateful for that.

The next morning, I settled into my couch, FaceTiming Tremaine and Dana for our usual debrief.

Tremaine smirked as she sipped her mimosa. "Okay, so spill. Did James top the helicopter ride or what?"

I rolled my eyes playfully. "You're not gonna believe this: He took me to a private Eric Roberson concert in a penthouse suite."

Dana's jaw dropped. "Girl, shut up. *Eric Roberson?*"

I nodded, smirking. "Turns out he's friends with James."

Tremaine gave me a pointed look. "See? That's some grown-man dating. But you still got that guarded energy. What's up?"

I sighed, leaning back. "I don't know. He's incredible, thoughtful, charming, but something about how meticulously he plans everything makes me pause. It's like he's orchestrating every moment, and I can't tell if it's genuine or just how he operates."

Dana nodded. "I get it. It's like, is he trying to impress you, or is he trying to control the dynamic?"

"Exactly." I rubbed my temples. "I don't want to sound ungrateful, but I need to figure out if this is real before I let my guard down."

Tremaine smirked. "Well, at least you got options. What about Robert?"

I groaned. "Oh, girl, don't even get me started. I still feel like something's off with him. He's charming, too, but I don't trust him. There's just something..."

Dana chuckled. "And yet, here you are entertaining both of them."

I laughed. "I'm dating. Exploring my options. Not committing to anything yet."

Tremaine raised her glass. "Well, cheers to that. But Joanie, be careful. Grand gestures don't always mean grand intentions."

I turned the focus to them. "Enough about me. What's been going on with y'all?"

Tremaine sighed dramatically. "Oh, girl, where do I start? Malik. Veronica. Max. A whole mess."

Dana and I leaned in. "Veronica?" I asked.

"Yeah. Turns out Malik has a wife, and she's one of Joanie's gallery clients. Can you believe that? And Max? He won't stop texting me. I think I'm officially done with men—at least, that's what I'm saying for now."

Dana chuckled, but then her smile faltered. "Honestly? I've been thinking about therapy."

I sat up straighter. "Therapy?"

Dana nodded. "With everything going on with Trey, I feel like I'm losing myself. I love him, I really do, but I need to figure out how to navigate this without losing me in the process."

Tremaine and I exchanged a glance before I spoke. "Dana, that makes so much sense. And you know we got you, right?"

Dana smiled, but it was laced with exhaustion. "I know, and I appreciate y'all more than you know."

I sighed, rubbing my temples. "I have so much going on right now. My event is coming up, and there are still so many details that my daughters and I have to firm up. After the next outing—the one in Houston with Robert—I'm going to have to really focus and reel things in, making sure my efforts go toward pulling off a successful event. Thank God my girls have got it, and I've trained them on pretty much everything there is to know about hosting it."

Dana smirked. "What about Robert and James? Are they privy to the event? Will you invite them?"

I scoffed, shaking my head. "Girl, I don't even know. I mean, I'd love for them to see what I'm passionate about, but I also don't want to feel like I'm showcasing my personal life in a professional setting. It's a fine line."

Tremaine leaned in with a sly grin. "This should be interesting."

Dana raised an eyebrow. "Well, it's not like it'll be a date with either of them. Your event isn't about them. No one is going to be babysitting their egos or their feelings. If they decide to come, they better bring a checkbook or whatever they use to donate because that's the only reason they should be there."

"I'll drink to that," Tremaine said, lifting her mimosa.

I shrugged, exhaling. "But you know it's a public event. It's been advertised on all the local news outlets—TV, radio, social media, all over town. It's open to everyone who can fit in the venue, so it would be hard *not* to inform them about it."

Our call ended. I sat back, reflecting. We were all navigating different struggles, different lessons, and different paths. But at the core of it, we still had each other.

Chapter 32

Joanie: Signs We Ignore

I sat at my desk in the gallery, staring at my laptop screen, my coffee growing cold beside me. Something about Robert just wasn't sitting right with me. The man was charming, intelligent, well-spoken, but those inconsistencies in his stories gnawed at me. I wasn't one to ignore my intuition, and right now, it was screaming at me.

I hesitated for a moment before typing his name into Google. At first, it was the usual—a LinkedIn profile, a few business features, a mention in a faculty directory. Then, an article caught my eye—a feature from a few years ago in an industry magazine. My breath caught as I read.

...Robert Whitmore, a proud father of three...

I blinked, reading it again. *Three?* He told me he had two sons. Two. Where was the third child in all of this?

A strange chill ran down my spine, but I shook it off and continued my search. Another article. An interview in a local business journal where he spoke about balancing his career and family life.

...Having been married twice and raising three wonderful children...

I swallowed hard. *Married twice?* I thought he had been married once. Or was that my assumption?

I leaned back in my chair, exhaling sharply. Why lie? And if he wasn't lying, why omit such major details? What else was he conveniently leaving out?

I picked up my phone and dialed Tremaine.

"Girl, I just found out some shit," I said as soon as she answered.

"Oh Lord." She sighed dramatically. "What now?"

I rubbed my temple. "Robert's been married twice, not once, and he has three kids, not two."

Tremaine let out a low whistle. "Damn. You sure?"

"Girl, I literally just read two separate articles where he said it himself. And the crazy part? He's never mentioned a third kid at all. Why omit something like that?"

"Because men love to lie," Tremaine said flatly. "They tell half-truths to make themselves look good, and before you know it, they've got you believing some bullshit version of reality."

I sighed. "I want to believe maybe he just didn't think it was relevant yet, but come on. Kids? Marriages? That's major. And we just talked about honesty—half-truths, omissions, all of it. And now this? Why is telling the truth so damn hard for them?"

Tremaine laughed dryly. "We always pray and ask God to send us signs, and when He does, what do we do? Ignore the hell out of them."

I shook my head, smirking despite my frustration. "Exactly. Then we sit up talking about, 'Lord, give me a clearer sign.' And God is like, 'What else do I need to do? Knock you upside the damn head with a brick?'"

Tremaine cackled. "Bitch, we got the signs. We just ignore them for the temporary feel-good."

I groaned. "*Whew.* You just read me my own damn truth."

"Look," Tremaine said, her voice softening. "If you don't feel right about it, trust that. You don't owe him anything. You like Robert, but you don't love him. You barely even know him. And if he's lying about basic shit this early? Just imagine what's next."

I let out a deep breath. "I know. But I really wanted to go to Houston. I mean, that exhibit is going to be amazing, and I was actually looking forward to the trip."

Tremaine hummed. "Bitch, so there you go, ignoring the truth for some dumb shit. Then go. But don't go as a woman who's being wooed—go as a woman who's got her eyes wide open. No blinders."

"You know what? You make a damn good point, girl," I admitted, surrendering to Tremaine's unfiltered truth. That was what I loved most about her—she never hesitated to say the things we all thought but were too afraid to speak aloud. Tremaine was like having my boldest, most reckless alter ego standing right in front of me, saying the things I needed to hear at the exact moment I needed to hear them.

Maybe, just maybe, it was time I stopped ignoring the signs I had prayed and asked God for. And maybe it was time I took some risks. After all, life is about taking chances.

I exhaled, shaking my head. "Yeah, you make a damn good point, girl," I said, finally giving in to Tremaine's unadulterated truth. God's truth wasn't exactly front and center here, but I'd deal with that later. Guess I'd suffer the consequences later—as usual.

Chapter 33

Tremaine: A Time of Reflection

It had been several weeks since the whole blow-up with Malik at my place. He had been texting and calling, trying to reconnect, but I ignored every attempt. I thought about blocking him, but curiosity got the better of me. I wanted to see if he would keep trying, if he would fight for my attention. But every time his name flashed across my screen, my stomach twisted with anger.

The worst part? I wasn't even sure why I was so mad. Was it because he had lied by omission, or was it because I had let myself get caught up again, despite knowing better?

I took a slow sip of my morning coffee, letting the warmth settle in my chest as I gazed out the window. The view was serene—my covered patio bathed in soft sunlight, the built-in grill standing untouched, and the pristine pool reflecting the sky like a perfect mirror.

I have so much to be grateful for.

There was a time when I loved my life, even when it was chaotic. Being a professor at the university meant there was never a dull moment—drama unfolded in real time, whether in the classroom, faculty meetings, or tangled office politics.

But now, the stillness of this morning felt more like a reminder than a reward.

The sharp ring of my phone cut through my thoughts. I glanced at the screen and sighed. *Pastor Kim.* That's what I called her when I was feeling sarcastic—my sister, the holy roller with a hotline to Jesus. Again.

I picked up with a groan. "What now, Kim? Trying to save my soul again?"

Her laughter was soft but knowing. "I wouldn't say save, exactly. More like gently redirect."

I smirked, swirling the last bit of coffee in my cup. "Redirect me where? To a pew in the front row while the ushers fan me down? Not happening."

Kim sighed dramatically. "Tremaine, I just called to check on you. No sermons. No scripture. Just me, your sister."

I leaned back into my chair. "No Bible-thumping? This is new."

"I mean it," she said, her tone softer this time. "I know you've been going through it, and I just want to be here for you."

I exhaled, letting my guard down just a little. "I know. And I appreciate it."

There was a pause before she spoke again. "You know, you can come to church with me anytime. No pressure. Just when you're ready."

I almost snorted. "Sis, you do realize I had a meltdown a few weeks ago, right? I almost went to church, but let's be real—I had way too many glasses of wine the night before. Church just didn't seem like the right timing."

Kim chuckled. "*Uh-huh,* or maybe you're just making excuses. Maybe you're afraid to face some things."

I stared at my coffee. "Maybe. Or maybe I just don't feel like dealing with judgment right now."

"Tremaine, it's not about judgment. It's about healing."

That word stuck with me. Healing. Was I healing or just numbing myself with distractions?

I sighed. "Look, I know you mean well. And I have been thinking about some things. Maybe therapy."

Kim gasped. "Wait, you—Tremaine 'I Don't Need Nobody' Johnson—are considering therapy?"

I rolled my eyes. "See, this is why I don't tell you things."

"No, no," Kim said, laughing. "I'm proud of you. Therapy is real, sis. And if you're even thinking about it, that's a step."

"Don't get too excited," I warned. "I haven't exactly signed up."

"Well, you should. Talking to someone outside your circle—someone neutral—it's a game-changer."

I mulled that over but kept it to myself. Instead, I changed the subject. "How's Mom?"

"She's good. Asked about you, as always. Said you need to come by more often."

I smiled, despite myself. "Yeah, yeah. I'll see about that."

"Alright, well, I'll let you go," Kim said. "Just think about what I said."

After we hung up, I found myself staring at my reflection in the mirror. Maybe Kim was right. Maybe I did need to do some soul-searching. Dana had been talking about therapy lately, wondering if she could benefit from it. Maybe I needed to take a page out of her book.

But instead of thinking about therapy, I thought about Max. And his other women. And the fact that, for the first time in a long while, I didn't even feel like playing the game anymore. I was tired. Exhausted, actually.

Maybe it was time to take my own advice. Maybe I should get on one of those dating apps and meet someone entirely new. Joanie had lucked out with two promising prospects—well, maybe one of them was promising. But did I really have the energy to go through all that?

Or maybe, just maybe, I needed a sabbatical from men altogether.

At least I had something positive to look forward to. Joanie and her daughters' art fundraiser scholarship event was coming up, and I was actually excited about it. A night of art, culture, and purpose. A night where I didn't have to think about Max, Malik, or any other man.

For once, that sounded like exactly what I needed.

Chapter 34

Joanie: The Last Straw

I gripped the steering wheel a little tighter than necessary as I made my way through the late-afternoon Dallas traffic. My mind was a battlefield of conflicting thoughts, but one thing was crystal clear: I had had it with Robert.

I should've trusted my gut. From the moment those inconsistencies started creeping into our conversations, I should have known better. The half-truths. The omissions. The way he told me just enough to keep me satisfied but never enough to give me the whole picture.

The more I thought about it, the more I realized that this wasn't just about Robert—it was about me. About the patterns I had allowed in my past. About Jackson and the way I let him string me along for far too long.

I exhaled sharply, shaking my head as I turned onto the street where the café was. *Never again.*

The memories of Jackson's bullshit were still fresh in my mind, no matter how much time had passed. How many times had I ignored my instincts with him? How many times had I rationalized his behavior, convincing myself that I was overthinking, that I was being too hard on him?

And where had that gotten me? Wasted years. Wasted emotions. A hard lesson learned.

The final straw had come when I saw those pictures of him grinning ear to ear with another woman—the same man who had spent years feeding me vague, noncommittal excuses about why we couldn't be more serious. And here he was, looking every bit the devoted partner to someone else.

That was the moment my illusion shattered. The moment I had woken up.

So, when Jackson texted me the other morning, I didn't hesitate. I didn't overthink it. I didn't fall into old habits.

I had typed out my response with steady hands and a clear mind: *Jackson, I'm no longer available. Not now. Not ever. I wish you well, but there's nothing left for us to discuss. Take care.*

And I meant every single word.

Just the thought of him now was enough to make my stomach turn. Not out of pain, not out of longing—but out of sheer disgust that I had allowed myself to be played for so long.

I was grateful to have healed from that chapter of my life.

I was grateful to be moving on.

Which is why I refused to walk into another situation with a man who couldn't be upfront with me.

Robert.

I sighed, slowing to park outside the café. Part of me wanted to just turn around and avoid this conversation altogether. But I wasn't that woman anymore.

No more making excuses. No more convincing myself that things were better than they actually were.

Robert needed to be confronted. And I needed to walk away before I let history repeat itself.

I took one last deep breath, adjusted my purse strap, and stepped out of the car.

It was time to say goodbye to another wrong choice.

I stared at my reflection in the café window, watching the condensation from my latte swirl in the cup. I had called this meeting—not to argue, not to accuse—but to get to the truth.

Robert walked in with his usual effortless charm, wearing that damn tailored blazer that screamed, *Trust me, I'm a good man*. I used to love that about him—how put together he always was, like a man who had his entire life figured out.

But now, I wasn't so sure.

"Hey, beautiful," he said smoothly, leaning in to kiss my cheek before taking his seat across from me.

I offered a small smile but didn't return the usual warmth. He noticed.

"Everything okay?" he asked, tilting his head.

I exhaled and set my cup down carefully. "Robert, I need to ask you something, and I want the truth. No sugarcoating, no smoothing things over. Just the truth."

His brows furrowed slightly, but he nodded. "Of course."

I leaned forward, keeping my voice calm but firm. "I did a little reading the other day. You've done some great interviews, really impressive." I paused, watching his reaction. "In one of them, you mentioned having three children."

Silence. His face barely twitched, but there it was—the flicker of surprise, the brief hesitation before the smooth talk would begin.

He cleared his throat. "Oh...that." He chuckled like I had caught him forgetting to take out the trash, not omitting a whole child. "I guess I never mentioned my eldest son. He and I...well, we're not as close as I'd like to be."

I nodded slowly, processing that. "And the two marriages?"

Another pause. This one longer.

He sighed, rubbing his jaw. "Joanie, I wasn't trying to deceive you. My past is just that—my past. I didn't think it was necessary to bring up things that have no bearing on us."

I scoffed. "No bearing on us? Robert, your children and your marriages are part of who you are. It's not about the past—it's about who I'm getting involved with."

He leaned forward, lowering his voice. "Listen, I care about you, Joanie. I didn't tell you because I didn't want to push you away before you got to know me for who I am now."

I let out a humorless laugh. "So, let me get this straight: You think lying by omission is a better foundation than honesty?"

His jaw tightened. "It wasn't a lie—"

"Robert." I held up a hand, my patience wearing thin. "You had multiple opportunities to be upfront. And you didn't. Instead, I had to find out on my own. That's a red flag, and you know it."

He sighed and leaned back, as if regrouping. "Joanie, I don't want to lose you over a misunderstanding."

I shook my head, my voice soft but firm. "It's not a misunderstanding, Robert. It's a pattern."

I picked up my bag and stood, feeling lighter than I had in weeks. Maybe even months.

He stood, too, reaching for my hand. "So, what are you saying?"

I exhaled, looking him in the eye. "I'm saying I need time, and if I can't trust what you say now, how can I trust anything else moving forward?"

I turned to leave, but before I walked out, I paused. "Oh, and by the way, I still plan to go to Houston, but not with you."

And with that, I walked out, leaving the inconsistencies—and Robert—behind.

Chapter 35

Tremaine: Baby Steps

I sat cross-legged on my bed, my laptop open in front of me, my fingers hovering over the keyboard. *African-American therapist near me. Virtual sessions available.* I hit enter and watched as a long list of names and practices filled the screen.

My stomach twisted. Therapy.

I had spent years dismissing the idea, convincing myself I didn't need some stranger dissecting my thoughts and picking apart my life choices. But after everything—the mess with Malik, the history with Max, and the ongoing war with myself—I had to admit, maybe I needed to talk to someone.

Baby steps, I reminded myself.

I wasn't committing to anything long-term. Just a session or two. A way to get my thoughts in order.

I clicked through a few profiles, reading bios, looking for a therapist who felt like the right fit. Someone sharp, someone no-nonsense. Someone who wouldn't feed me sugar-coated affirmations but would actually call me on my bullshit.

Before I could bookmark a name, my phone rang. *Joanie.*

I reached for it, pressing the speaker button as I got up and started rummaging through my closet.

"Hey, girl," I answered, pulling out a deep red dress, then shaking my head and tossing it aside.

"Hey yourself," Joanie said, her voice carrying that mix of relief and exhaustion that told me something had gone down. "You busy?"

"Trying to find something to wear to church this Sunday," I said casually, flipping through my hangers.

Joanie choked. "Wait. What? Did you just say church?"

I smirked. "You heard me."

"Hold on. Let me sit down. I need to process this," she teased. "Because you, Miss I Ain't Stepping Foot in No Church, are voluntarily going?"

I rolled my eyes. "Look, before you start planning my baptism, it's just one Sunday. They're doing a whole dating-over-fifty panel, and I may have been watching their online service a little."

Joanie gasped. "You've been watching?"

"Don't make a big deal out of it," I warned. "It's not that serious. But I figure since Kim won't shut up about me going, I might as well show up for this one."

Joanie hummed knowingly. "So you're warming up to the idea?"

I sighed, pulling a navy blue dress off the rack. "Let's just say I'm open. Baby steps."

"Well, look at you," Joanie said, amusement in her voice. "Next thing I know, you'll be in a Bible study group."

"Now, let's not get carried away," I shot back.

Joanie laughed, then her voice shifted, turning more serious. "Listen, I called because I need to vent. I finally confronted Robert."

I froze mid-motion. "Oh shit. What happened?"

Joanie launched into the whole play-by-play, from the moment Robert sat down across from her to the moment she walked out on him.

"Damn," I said when she finished. "I knew there was something off about him. And girl, I'm so glad you trusted your instincts. That could've been a whole mess."

"Right?" Joanie sighed. "And look, I still want to go to Houston for the Kinsey exhibit, but not with him, so I had an idea. Let's make it a girls' trip—you, me, and Dana."

I smirked, tossing the navy dress on my bed. "I like the sound of that."

"Right? It'll be fun and relaxing. Art has a way of doing that for the psyche."

I nodded, even though she couldn't see me. "Dana might need a break, too, with everything going on with Trey. You think she'll be down?"

"Honestly, I don't know," Joanie admitted. "I don't want to pull her away when she and Trey are going through so much, but at the same time, maybe she needs it. We'll see how she's feeling."

"Yeah, well, if Dana can't go, we'll make it a duo trip," I said. "Either way, I'm in."

Joanie exhaled, like a weight had lifted. "Good. Because, girl, I need a damn reset after all this Robert mess."

I chuckled, sitting on my bed. "Houston it is then. Let me know when you wanna book."

"Will do. Oh, and Tremaine?"

"Yeah?"

She paused, then said, "Proud of you for doing the therapy search and for going to church."

I smirked, shaking my head. "Don't make a big deal out of it."

Joanie laughed. "Too late."

I rolled my eyes, but I couldn't help the small smile tugging at my lips. Maybe, just maybe, baby steps were exactly what I needed.

As soon as I hung up, my phone buzzed again. I expected to see Joanie's name.

But it wasn't her.

It was Max.

And he wasn't just texting.

He was calling.

I stared at the screen, my stomach twisting. *Baby steps,* I reminded myself.

But some steps led right back into old mistakes.

Chapter 36

Dana: A Load Lifted

I stood at the kitchen sink, staring blankly at the running water as it filled my glass teapot. The rhythmic hum of the dishwasher in the background was the only noise in the house aside from Trey's faint breathing from the bedroom. He had been knocked out since last night, the effects of his latest treatment leaving him drained. I knew he needed the rest, but it didn't make watching him like this any easier.

I took a slow sip of my chamomile tea, letting the warmth settle inside me, but it didn't do much to ease the fatigue that sat heavy in my bones.

I was tired.

Not just physically, but emotionally. Mentally. Spiritually.

Our boys had called earlier to check in, and I had put on my best everything-is-fine voice for them. They didn't live at home anymore, and as much as I wanted them to drop everything and be here, I knew that wasn't fair. They had their own lives. So, I smiled through the phone, reassured them their father was doing as well as expected, and told them I had everything under control.

But the truth?

I didn't feel like I had anything under control.

I leaned against the counter, rubbing my temples. This was the in-sickness-and-in-health part, I reminded myself. The part you don't think about when you're standing at the altar, staring into your spouse's eyes, promising forever. The part you don't imagine when you're young and in love, thinking the hard times will be arguments over finances or where to spend the holidays.

But this?

I sure as hell didn't see this coming.

It had been weeks since Trey's confession. The weight of his words still sat in my chest like a stone.

"Dana, I need to tell you something. It's nothing that went too far, but..."

I had felt it before he even said it. That gut-punch instinct.

He had been flirting with a new intern.

The moment those words left his mouth, my whole world tilted.

He swore up and down it was nothing. That it was never physical, just friendly conversation that he later realized had crossed a line. That he had never been unfaithful to me in any real way, and his therapist had encouraged him to be honest before it became something more.

But honesty hadn't made it sting any less.

I had been carrying that revelation alone. Hadn't told Tremaine or Joanie. Hadn't breathed a word of it to anyone. Because what was I supposed to say? That my husband, the man I had stood by for decades, the one I was now nursing through his hardest season, had entertained the idea of something new? That even as he faced one of the toughest battles of his life, he still had a moment where he...what? Needed validation from someone else?

It made me sick.

I wasn't ready to process it, so I buried it. Pushed it aside. Focused on taking care of Trey, being the strong wife, the dependable mother.

But lately, I had been questioning everything.

I was so happy for Joanie and Tremaine, but I also envied them more than I cared to admit. Their freedom. Their ability to just pick up and go, to date without attachments, to experience new things.

I loved Trey. I loved my life. I wouldn't trade my family for anything, but sometimes, just sometimes, I wondered.

My phone rang, breaking my thoughts. I exhaled deeply, walking over to pick it up. Joanie.

I answered with a little more enthusiasm than I felt. "Hey, girl."

"Hey. You busy?"

I glanced toward the bedroom, where Trey was still sleeping. "No. Just having some tea."

Joanie sighed, and I could tell instantly that something was up.

"What's wrong?" I asked.

"Girl, Robert. He's full of it."

I grabbed my mug and sat down, letting Joanie spill everything—the lies, the half-truths, the final confrontation.

I shook my head. "Damn. So, you're really done with him?"

"Oh, absolutely," Joanie said without hesitation. "But listen, I still want to go to Houston for the Kinsey exhibit, just not with him, so I had an idea: Let's make it a girls' trip—you, me, and Tremaine."

A slow smile pulled at my lips. "A girls' trip?"

"Yep," Joanie said. "I know things are crazy with Trey, so I don't want to impose or take you away if you're needed, but I also know you might need this, so I wanted to extend the invite."

I took a deep breath, chewing on my bottom lip.

"You deserve this, Dana," Joanie added gently.

She was right.

I did need this.

Trey would be fine, and honestly, this would be a perfect time for the boys to step up.

"I'll talk to the boys and tell them they need to come spend some time with their dad," I said, already making up my mind. "They need to be here anyway, and I think it'll be good for all of us."

Joanie cheered. "Yes! That's what I'm talking about! This trip is exactly what we all need—something refreshing, inspiring, drama-free."

I chuckled. "You do realize Tremaine is coming, right? Drama-free might be a stretch."

Joanie laughed. "Fair. But at least it won't be our drama."

I exhaled, feeling the weight in my chest loosen just a little. "You know what? Count me in. I need this."

"Good," Joanie said. "Now go make sure you got some badass outfits ready because you know we gotta show out."

I smiled for the first time in what felt like forever.

Maybe this was exactly what I needed.

As soon as I hung up, I turned toward the bedroom and froze.

Trey was awake.

And he was staring at me.

Chapter 37

Joanie: Unexpected Connections

The scent of fresh espresso filled the gallery as I adjusted a new canvas on display. The morning had been a whirlwind, but I was looking forward to lunch with my girls. Houston was officially happening, and after all the drama lately, we needed a break.

I checked my watch. Dana and Tremaine should be arriving any minute.

Right on cue, the door chimed. Tremaine strolled in first, exuding effortless confidence in a linen jumpsuit, her signature bold lipstick making a statement. Dana followed, looking as polished as ever, though her tired eyes betrayed how much she'd been dealing with.

"Alright, ladies," I said, stepping toward them. "We are officially one week away from Houston. Are y'all ready for this?"

Tremaine smirked. "Baby, I stay ready. It's Dana we gotta worry about."

Dana shot her a look before exhaling. "Look, I need this trip. I've been playing nurse, therapist, and referee all at once. A little art, some wine, and good company sounds like heaven right now."

I smiled, but before I could respond, the gallery door chimed again.

I turned automatically, expecting another client, but the second I saw her, my stomach twisted.

Veronica.

She walked in like she owned the damn place, her head held high, her outfit impeccable. Poised. Polished. Dangerous.

I knew she wasn't just here for art.

"Joanie," she said smoothly, sauntering toward me with a smirk that set off every alarm in my body.

Tremaine and Dana were still mid-conversation, oblivious.

I turned quickly to them. "Ladies, go ahead and grab a seat in the back. I just need to take care of something real quick."

Tremaine barely glanced up, distracted by a sculpture. "We got time, girl. Take care of your client."

I could feel Veronica watching me, that knowing glint in her eyes. Damn it, Malik must have filled her in. My women's intuition kicked in full gear.

Veronica folded her arms. "Oh, they don't have to leave. Actually, I'd love to meet your friends."

I stiffened.

Oh, hell no.

"Maybe another time," I said, keeping my voice even.

Veronica tilted her head, amused. "Oh, I insist. After all, I already know so much about them."

My pulse jumped.

Before I could stop her, Tremaine's head snapped up like she'd just sensed something was off.

Dana, who had been casually scrolling through her phone, finally caught on to the shift in energy. She looked up, glancing between me and Veronica. "*Uh*...what's going on?"

Veronica smirked. "I was just hoping to introduce myself since we're all connected in a way."

Connected?

Tremaine narrowed her eyes, stepping forward. "I don't think we've met. You are...?"

I inhaled sharply, about to intervene, but Veronica beat me to it.

"Veronica," she said, extending a perfectly manicured hand. "Malik's wife."

Silence.

The words seemed to freeze the entire damn room.

Tremaine blinked once. Then twice. Processing.

Dana gasped softly. "Wait. What?"

I felt my stomach twist. This was exactly what I wanted to avoid.

Then, as expected, Tremaine lost it.

She let out a long, dramatic sigh before letting her purse drop on to the counter. "Oh, well ain't this some bullshit."

Dana's mouth flung open as she looked between all of us. "Okay. Somebody better start talking because I feel like I just walked into a damn episode of *Scandal*."

Tremaine turned her gaze to me. Her voice was dangerously calm. "Joanie, you knew about this?"

I opened my mouth, then closed it.

There was no easy way to explain how I'd figured it out before she did.

Veronica was enjoying this way too much. She crossed her arms, eyes flicking toward Tremaine. "I see Malik didn't tell you."

Tremaine slowly turned back to her, tilting her head. "Tell me what exactly?"

Veronica's smirk widened. "That he wants out."

Tremaine blinked. "Come again?"

"Malik," Veronica said smoothly, "is realizing that this whole polyamory thing isn't for him. I could've told him that from the start, but some men have to learn the hard way, you know?"

Tremaine sucked her teeth. "Girl, if you don't get all the way the hell outta my face with that mess."

Veronica chuckled, shaking her head. "Relax, Tremaine. I'm not here to fight over a man. I just wanted to see for myself who had him so conflicted."

Tremaine's laugh was cold. "Well, congratulations. Now you've seen me. Now you can bounce."

Veronica's smirk faltered, but she recovered quickly. "I just hope you're prepared for the fallout."

Tremaine crossed her arms. "Fallout? Honey, I don't do fallout. Malik ain't my man. He was a good time. That's it. And quite frankly, I've been over it and him."

Veronica studied her for a long moment, as if trying to determine whether or not she was telling the truth. Then she exhaled dramatically and turned toward me.

"Lovely gallery, Joanie. I'll be sure to recommend it."

And just like that, she turned and walked out, leaving a storm of tension behind her.

The second the door closed, Tremaine turned to me with murder in her eyes. "Joanie. Explain."

I sighed, rubbing my temple. "It's a long story."

Tremaine picked up her purse and slung it over her shoulder. "Girl, I got time."

I exhaled, raising both hands in surrender. "Tremaine, I swear to you, I had nothing to do with that mess."

Dana, still standing shell-shocked, let out a breath. "Okay. Wait. So that was Malik's wife?" She looked at me. "And you knew?"

I pinched the bridge of my nose. "I figured it out recently. I didn't tell you because honestly, I didn't think it mattered. Malik wasn't my business, and Tremaine had already been done with him." I looked at Tremaine. "But, girl, I did not set that up. She came in here as a client. She called the other day saying she wanted to look at some new pieces. I didn't even think twice about it."

Tremaine folded her arms. "And it just so happened I was here today?"

I shook my head. "I don't know how she knew. It could've been a fluke, or maybe Malik said something that tipped her off. But what I do know: That woman came in here with a damn agenda."

Tremaine sucked her teeth, shaking her head. "And you mean to tell me that bitch put all that effort into orchestrating this little scene? Girl, please," she scoffed. "Maybe Malik does want out, and this is her way of retaliating. But guess what? I. Do. Not. Care."

Dana let out a low whistle. "*Whew,* Jesus."

Tremaine turned to her. "No, for real, Dana. You know what's crazy? This little girl really thought she had me." She let out a bitter laugh. "Like I was about to argue over some man-child who's still out here figuring out his emotions like a damn eighth grader."

Dana smirked. "I mean...the dramatics of it all. We can't even go to lunch without getting ambushed."

Tremaine shook her head. "You know what I really ain't got time for?" She raised a hand, ticking the points off on her fingers. "First of all, I ain't got time to be part of some messy-ass love triangle. Second, I ain't got time to be lied to by either of them. And third—" She paused, inhaling deeply, "that bitch is lucky I am not the woman I used to be because back in the day? *Whew...*"

I felt a shiver go through me as I saw the old Tremaine flash behind her eyes for a split second.

"Girl..." Dana whispered, looking nervous.

Tremaine narrowed her eyes at the door, as if still picturing Veronica standing there. "They would've been cleaning up blood and figuring out what to do with her body."

Dana gasped. "Tremaine!"

Tremaine held up a hand. "I ain't saying I would've done it today! I'm just saying—" She sighed dramatically. "That used to be my energy. But I'm too damn grown for that now. I got peace to protect."

I bit my lip, suppressing a smirk. "So, you definitely don't care what Malik wants?"

Tremaine snapped her head back to me. "Joanie." She placed a hand on her hip. "I do not give a single solitary fuck about what Malik wants."

Dana, still recovering, plopped down onto one of the gallery's display chairs and let out an exhausted breath. "*Whew*, girl. Joanie, tell me you've got something strong in the back to drink."

I chuckled. "I do, but it's a little early."

Dana waved a hand. "Early where? It's five o'clock somewhere, baby."

Tremaine let out a short laugh, then exhaled, rolling her shoulders back. "You know what? Forget them. Forget this whole incident. Let's eat, and then, let's go shopping. We need outfits for Houston."

I nodded, finally relieved to see Tremaine moving past it.

Dana stood. "That's the first logical thing I've heard all damn day. Let's go."

As we left the gallery, the weight of the drama lifted slightly, but I couldn't shake the feeling that something told me we hadn't heard the last from Veronica...or Malik.

Chapter 38

Joanie: Deep-Tissue Massages and Deeper Conversations

The moment we stepped into the Four Seasons Houston, I exhaled deeply, taking in the opulence that surrounded us. Plush velvet seating in the lobby, a stunning chandelier overhead, and the subtle scent of luxury that whispered, *This is exactly where you belong.*

"Now this...this is what I call treating ourselves," Tremaine said, slipping her sunglasses off and glancing around.

Dana rolled her shoulders back. "Listen, I love my husband, but this? This is the kind of luxury I could get used to on a regular basis."

We checked into our suite, a sprawling two-bedroom masterpiece overlooking the city skyline. Every inch of the place screamed elegance—from the floor-to-ceiling windows to the oversized soaking tubs. This weekend wasn't just about art. It was about us.

And first on the agenda? The spa.

We sprawled out on heated massage tables, the scent of lavender and eucalyptus filling the dimly lit room. Soft instrumental jazz played in the background, but the real conversation? That was happening between us.

The massage therapist had barely started working out the knots in my back when Dana's voice cut through the relaxed silence.

"Okay, real talk," she said, letting out a deep breath as she sank farther into the table. "What is something you constantly see me struggle with that you hope I finally learn to work through or just let go of?"

Tremaine chuckled. "Damn, Dana. Can we ease into the deep shit?"

Dana laughed softly. "Nope. We're here, we're relaxed. Let's talk."

I thought about it for a moment before responding. "Honestly? Balance. You take on everything—Trey, your sons, your job, keeping your household in order. You're always on, and I just want to see you do something for you—without guilt."

Dana sighed. "I hear you, but how do I do that? If I don't take care of things, who will?"

Tremaine piped up. "Girl, trust me, I get it. But when exactly do you come first? At what point do you say, *I deserve to put myself at the top of the list*?"

Dana was quiet for a moment before whispering, "I don't know."

The weight of her admission settled between us.

Then Tremaine groaned, shifting slightly on her table. "Alright. Since we're laying shit bare, let me put my mess on the table. What do y'all see me struggling with?"

I smirked. "Control."

Dana snorted. "Facts."

Tremaine laughed, but I knew she knew we were serious.

I continued, "You don't like to admit when something bothers you until it explodes. You'll hold it in, pretend it's nothing, and then—*boom*—you go off like a damn grenade."

Tremaine sighed dramatically. "You might be a little right."

I grinned. "Girl, puleeze. You know we're right."

I sank deeper into the warmth of the massage table, the sheets wrapping around me like a cocoon. The dim lights and gentle scent of lavender made it easy to let go. I glanced to my left—Tremaine was still chatting with her therapist, probably asking if they had strong hands. Typical. A moment later, I heard her say to her therapist, "Okay now, don't be shy, dig in like you mean it," already cracking a joke.

Dana, in her usual composed way, ever the graceful one, let out a slow, contented sigh from the other side of us. "This," she said softly, "is exactly what I needed." We were finally still, each of us in our own world, but together in the same peaceful space. Despite the tranquility, our conversation took a more personal turn.

Dana, her voice gentle yet probing, added to the silence. "You know, Tre, given further thought, I've noticed that whenever things get a bit too real, you whip out that sarcasm like it's your shield."

Tremaine let out a dramatic sigh, her tone playful. "Oh, come on. Me? Sarcastic? Never."

I chuckled softly, turning my head slightly toward Tremaine. "Girl, we've known each other too long. I can tell when you're using humor to deflect. It's like your superpower." Tremaine's tone faded, and her voice went quiet. Even with her face pressed into the cradle, I could feel the shift—like all the air had been sucked out of her usual sass. "Your kryptonite."

"I guess it's just easier, you know? Keeps things from getting too...messy."

Dana's voice softened further. "We get it. But remember, with us, this is your safe space. You don't always have to put on a brave face with us, and I think that sentiment is shared and vice versa."

Tremaine sighed. I sensed a mix of relief and vulnerability in her reply. "You might be a little right."

I grinned, though my face was nestled in the massage cradle. "Girl, Dana is speaking the truth up in here!"

We laughed, the tension easing as we embraced the comfort of our unbreakable bond.

Our conversation took a turn, and judging by the sudden pause in hands on my back and the subtle shift in the room's energy by my therapist, we were being too loud. One of the other therapists gently cleared their throat—a quiet cue. On key, our voices lowered. The therapists continued to work out the tension in our bodies. Then Dana spoke up again.

"What does it say about me if I keep expecting something to change in my relationship, and it doesn't?"

Silence.

The three of us lay on our massage tables listening to the soft music, the gentle aroma of essential oils creating a serene atmosphere as our conversation took a reflective turn.

Tremaine spoke up first, her voice thoughtful. "You know, they say if you want different results, you gotta do something you haven't done before. Otherwise, you'll just keep experiencing the same things."

Dana let out a contemplative hum. "I've never heard it put that way, Tremaine, but I get what you're saying."

Joanie added, "If it's a person you're talking about, you can't force them to change, especially if they're not willing to grow. That's the bottom line. If nothing changes, neither will your pain. In relationships, if you don't address the issues causing bad behavior, or if the person doesn't improve, you'll just keep accepting the same patterns."

Tremaine exhaled deeply. "So, it's up to you whether you choose to stay in that toxic cycle."

Dana nodded slowly. "Damn. Y'all are really giving me something to think about today."

We all shared a soft laugh, but the weight of our words lingered.

Tremaine didn't say a word, but I felt something change. I heard a slight creak from her table—nothing big, but I could feel a subtle shift in her body movement— it was enough to catch my attention. When you've been friends as long as we have, you don't need to see someone to know when their energy takes a turn. She hesitated as she spoke, her voice softer now. "Yeah, you gotta know when enough is enough and when to leave. It's as simple as that."

The gravity of her statement settled over me, as each of us reflected on our individual experiences.

Because we'd all been there.

Holding on too long. Ignoring red flags. Wasting time hoping someone would become the version of themselves we needed—instead of accepting them for who they actually were.

As we continued to lay on our massage tables, the room filled with a serene ambience, I decided to take advantage of the moment. "Since we're having this come-to-Jesus talk," I began hesitantly, "what's one thing you think I could work on?"

Without missing a beat, as if they'd rehearsed it, Dana and Tremaine responded in unison, "Trust."

Dana turned her head slightly toward me. "Joanie, you don't trust any man. You shut them down before they even get a chance to know you. I get vetting them out, but damn, girl, give a guy a chance."

Tremaine chimed in, her voice gentle yet firm. "It's like you've built these walls so high, nobody can climb them. Maybe it's time to let someone in, even just a little."

Their words hit me hard. Was I really that guarded? I prided myself on being independent, on protecting my heart, but maybe, just maybe, I was also keeping out the possibility of genuine connection. Their insights forced me to confront a truth I had been avoiding: Trust was not just about others earning it, but also about me being willing to give it.

As I lay there, the soothing hands of the massage therapist working away tension, I realized that if I wanted different results in my relationships, I needed to change my approach. Perhaps it was time to dismantle some of those walls and allow myself to be vulnerable, to trust—not just others, but also my own judgment.

The weight of their observations settled over me, blending with the physical relaxation of the massage. It was a lot to process, but I knew they were right. Change wouldn't be easy, but acknowledging the need for it was the first step.

We let the conversation settle. The massage therapists finished up. One thing was certain.

This trip?

It wasn't just about art and luxury.

It was about us.

Releasing.

Healing.

And finally, doing what was needed individually, collectively, and moving the hell on to what the next thing would be.

After our spa services concluded, we were guided to the dressing and shower areas to refresh. I found myself alone in my dressing area, the soft ambient music providing a soothing backdrop. A therapist handed me a small cup of herbal tea, its warmth seeping into my hands, mirroring the warmth of memories flooding my mind.

Tremaine, Dana, and I had been inseparable for decades, our bond forged in the crucible of life's challenges. At that time, each one of us had migrated to the metroplex from different parts of the Midwest. We met nearly thirty years ago at one of Dallas' local community center's wellness workshops. Tremaine, with her fiery spirit, was leading a session on self-empowerment, while Dana and I were attendees seeking solace and guidance. Our shared experiences and mutual support blossomed into a friendship that had weathered the storms of time.

As I sipped my tea, thoughts drifted to my past marriages, each leaving indelible marks on my soul. The first, a whirlwind romance I once believed I couldn't live without, ended abruptly when I discovered his infidelity. The betrayal cut deep, shattering my trust and leaving me questioning my worth. The second marriage, though initially promising, unraveled as lies surfaced, revealing a man who was not only a stranger beneath the surface but also battling substance abuse. Both experiences left me guarded, building walls to protect my heart from further pain. Yet, the silver lining was my beautiful daughters, Layla and Aisha. For their existence, I wouldn't change a single moment of those past relationships.

In the aftermath of those marriages, I sought therapy, hoping to understand and heal from the wounds they left behind. I believed I had done the work, fortified myself against future heartaches. But then came Jackson. I let my guard down, allowed myself to believe in the possibility of love again. His sudden disappearance after months of connection reopened old wounds, but this time, I chose a different path. Instead of retreating, I returned to therapy, delving deeper into the roots of my trust issues and learning to establish healthy boundaries.

Now, venturing into the uncharted territory of online dating, I found myself navigating connections with two men, James and Robert. Each carried his own aura of mystery, challenging me to apply the lessons I've learned. It's a delicate balance—remaining open to new possibilities while honoring the boundaries I'd set for myself.

Through introspection and the unwavering support of Tremaine and Dana, I continue to heal. I've come to understand that trust starts within, and by embracing my journey, I can open my heart to genuine connections. The path isn't easy, but it's one I walk with resilience and hope.

Chapter 39

Joanie: The Kinsey Exhibit: A History We Carry

I exhaled slowly as I took in the scene around me. The Kinsey African American Art & History Collection was more than an exhibit, it was a testament—a reminder of where we had been, what we had endured, and how much further we had to go.

Tremaine, Dana, and I moved through the space like women on a pilgrimage, stopping at each piece, allowing the weight of history to settle in our bones.

Tremaine lingered at an old, worn copy of *The Negro Motorist Green Book*, shaking her head. "Imagine having to carry this damn thing just to travel in your own country—having to map out where you could safely eat, sleep, breathe."

Dana sighed, arms crossed. "Tremaine, let's be real: The Lord knew what He was doing not birthing you during those times."

I smirked. "Facts."

Dana pointed at her. "Because, sis, you would've been arrested on sight. That mouth? That attitude? They'd have snatched you up quick."

Tremaine gasped dramatically, placing a hand on her chest. "Excuse me? First of all, I am a sweetheart—"

Dana and I gave her a side-eye so synchronized, you'd think we rehearsed it.

Tremaine rolled her eyes. "Fine. Maaaaybe I would've been a bit of a problem."

We chuckled, but the laughter was short-lived as we turned our attention to a framed, yellowed document.

A bill of sale—for a person.

I swallowed hard as my gaze trailed over the writing. A sixteen-year-old girl. Sold for four hundred dollars.

A silence fell over us.

Tremaine's voice was soft but firm. "History has shown us time and time again how critical it is to protect civil rights for everyone."

I nodded. "Because, let's be real: This ain't just history. It's still happening in different forms, just dressed up in modern clothes."

Dana exhaled sharply. "Just like Mamie Till said, 'What happens to any of us, anywhere in the world, had better be the business of us all.' And that's why we still have to fight."

I looked at both of them, emotion tightening my throat. "This is more than just an exhibit. It's a reminder. A call to action. It makes me feel like I'm not doing enough."

Tremaine nudged me. "Girl, please. You're out here changing lives with that scholarship program. That's more than most people ever do."

Dana nodded. "Yeah, Joanie, don't downplay that. What you're doing for those young girls is huge."

I smiled, touched by their words, but before I could respond, I saw someone who looked very familiar.

My breath caught in my throat.

David.

He hadn't changed much—not in the ways that mattered. Taller than I remembered, or maybe just standing a little prouder. He still carried that quiet confidence like it was stitched into his DNA, the kind that made girls lean in without realizing they were doing it. The years had been generous—just enough silver at his temples to mark time, but his face, his presence, still had that same pull. His smile hadn't dulled; it had only deepened, softened by time, sharpened by experience.

I literally thought my mind was playing tricks on me. I couldn't fathom seeing him here. We'd known each other way back—late high school, maybe early college. Those years blur when the feelings were fleeting, but the memory stays crisp. We never really had our moment, not all the way. Timing was off, or maybe life just stepped in and made the decision for us. He belonged to someone else back then, but that didn't stop him from showing up in the quiet corners of my mind over the years.

David had always been the kind of man who didn't ask for attention but got it anyway. And now, here he was again—stepping into the room like a memory I hadn't expected to see standing in full color.

I had almost convinced myself I was mistaken, but then—

Our eyes met.

I felt the heat creep up my neck. I knew he recognized me because his lips curved into that same damn grin I remembered from years ago.

Tremaine noticed the shift in my expression immediately. "*Uh-oh*. Who is that?"

Dana turned, eyes darting across the room. "Wait. Who? Where?"

Tremaine followed my gaze, then gasped dramatically. "Oh, hell no. Is that...is that a blast from the past?"

I straightened my posture. "Tremaine, please—"

Dana leaned in, eyes twinkling with mischief. "Girl, who is he?"

Tremaine snapped her fingers. "Spill it, Joanie. You know we love a good throwback."

I sighed, but a smirk tugged at my lips. "David. He was...well, let's just say he was a part of my early arts introduction."

Dana raised a brow. "Oh, so that kind of introduction?"

Tremaine gasped. "Wait. Is he the one?"

I groaned. "Oh my God, not here."

But before I could talk my way out of this, David started walking toward me.

Tremaine whisper-screamed, "Oh, this is about to get good."

Dana grabbed my wrist. "Okay. Do you need us to leave, stay, or fake a sudden emergency?"

I barely had time to answer before David was standing in front of me, grinning like he'd just stumbled upon a treasure he thought he'd lost.

"Joanie Williams."

His voice still had that smooth, deep tone I remembered.

I folded my arms. "David Carter. Well, look at you."

"Look at you," he countered. "Still stopping men in their tracks, I see."

Tremaine behind me snorted.

I cleared my throat, ignoring my nosy-ass friends. "What brings you here?"

David tucked his hands into his pockets. "I've been involved with the Kinsey Collection for years—helped curate a few pieces for this exhibit."

Of course he had.

He glanced over at my friends who were terrible at pretending they weren't eavesdropping.

"And you must be Joanie's security team."

Tremaine placed a hand on her hip. "Oh, honey, we're way more than security."

Dana smirked. "We're the vetting committee."

David chuckled. "Fair enough." He turned back to me. "I'd love to catch up. Maybe after the exhibit?"

Tremaine gasped dramatically, grabbing Dana's arm. "Did he just ask our girl out?"

Dana nodded solemnly. "He did."

I shot them both a look.

David smirked. "I see you've got a tough crowd."

I exhaled, tilting my head. "Alright, David. Let's catch up."

Tremaine whooped.

Dana clapped. "Oh, this is better than TV."

I shook my head, but deep down, I couldn't deny it. I was intrigued.

And maybe—just maybe—this trip to Houston was about to get very interesting.

The exhibit wound down. I found myself caught between nostalgia and curiosity. David Carter. Of all the places, of all the exhibits, of all the moments, I never expected to run into him.

I sat across from him at a dimly lit lounge not far from the museum, a jazz trio playing softly in the background. The conversation had been easy, flowing like it always had between us. No awkward pauses, no fumbling for words—just two old friends catching up on life.

David sipped his bourbon and smiled at me. "I still can't believe this. I've been looking for you."

I smirked, swirling my French 75 cocktail. A classic cocktail made with gin, lemon juice, simple syrup and champagne. "Believe what exactly? And what do you mean, you've been looking for me?"

"That I'm sitting here with you after all these years—forty years married. I've wondered how I could've gotten in touch with you, where you were, if you were married, all those things and there you were when I'd least expected it." He exhaled, shaking his head.

"Joanie, I don't think I've ever told you this, but back in college, I had the biggest crush on you."

I nearly choked on my drink. "Stop playing."

"I'm dead serious." He chuckled, leaning back. "You were so vibrant, so full of life, and, of course, out of my league."

I rolled my eyes. "Boy, please." In my mind, I thought, *So, it was during our college years.* The memory suddenly came back to me, clear as day.

He gave me a knowing look. "I mean it. But fate had other plans. My wife—God rest her soul—got pregnant right before I could even think about making a move, and well..." He shrugged. "The rest is history."

I softened. "I'm sorry about your wife. Forty years together—that's beautiful."

He nodded. "It was. She was my best friend, and when she passed, I couldn't imagine ever finding that kind of connection again." His eyes held mine. "Until today."

I felt my stomach flip but quickly took another sip of my cocktail. *Don't do this, Joanie. Don't get caught up.*

As David and I sat across from each other, the atmospheric hum of the lounge surrounding us, he shared more stories of his late wife and their life together. His openness was both comforting and intimidating.

David chuckled, shaking his head. "I can see that look in your eyes. You've been through some things."

I sighed, glancing down at my drink. "Yeah...you can say that."

He leaned forward, his gaze gentle yet probing. "I won't push. But just know, I'm not some man looking for a distraction. If life has taught me anything, it's that time is too damn short for games."

His honesty was refreshing—almost too refreshing. It was unsettling in the best and worst ways.

I felt a familiar tension rising within me—a hesitation to divulge too much, a fear rooted in past wounds. My previous marriages had left scars, teaching me to guard my feelings, to withhold parts of myself to avoid potential pain.

As I gazed into David's earnest eyes, a realization washed over me: If I desired genuine connection and honesty from him, I needed to offer the same in return. It was a daunting thought, but perhaps, after all these years, it was time to confront my fears and embrace vulnerability.

Reflecting further, I pondered my past entanglement with Jackson. If I had to be honest with myself, could it be that I allowed myself to get involved with him as a way to avoid true commitment? Maybe it was me all along who hadn't wanted any commitment. When I saw the pictures of him with someone else, it was more of a bruised ego and not so much anything else because deep down, I knew that what he and I had wasn't anything substantial. But now, I know I want and deserve so much more than that, and I understand what it takes to have it.

This introspection made me recognize that my fear of commitment had been a recurring theme in my relationships. I had often chosen partners who were emotionally unavailable or situations that lacked depth, perhaps as a way to protect myself from potential hurt. But with David, things felt different. His openness and sincerity challenged me to break free from my self-imposed barriers and to embrace the possibility of a deeper, more meaningful connection.

Determined to change, I decided it was time to let go of my past fears and to approach this new chapter with an open heart. I owed it to myself—and to David—to be fully present and to give this budding relationship the honesty and commitment it deserved.

We kept talking, unaware of how much time had passed until the lounge was nearly empty.

David glanced at his watch. "I should probably get you back before your security team calls a search party."

I laughed. "Oh, you have no idea."

The ride back to my hotel was filled with a comfortable silence, the kind that didn't need words. When we reached my door, David stood close but not too close, his presence steady, unhurried.

"I'd love to see you again," he said, his voice warm.

I hesitated, but then, for the first time in a long while, I made a choice without overthinking it. "I'd like that too."

A slow smile spread across his face. He reached for my hand, pressing a soft kiss to my knuckles before meeting my eyes. "Good night, Joanie."

"Good night, David."

I stepped inside, closing the door behind me and exhaling like I had been holding my breath the entire night.

And then...

"Bitch, what took you so long?!"

I turned to find Tremaine and Dana sitting on the hotel bed like two teenagers waiting for the tea.

I groaned, kicking off my heels. "Y'all need lives."

Tremaine smirked. "Nah. You need to spill the details."

Dana grinned, holding up a glass. "You know the rules. No information, no wine."

I sighed dramatically, grabbing a glass and plopping down in the chair. "Alright, alright. His name is David Carter, we went to college together, and yes, he still looks damn good."

Tremaine raised a brow. "*Mm-hmm*...and?"

"And," I continued, swirling my wine, "he's a widower. Married for forty years. Never remarried. And apparently, back in college, he had a thing for me."

Dana gasped. "What? Are you serious?"

Tremaine put a hand over her chest. "Oh, that's a romantic-ass plot twist."

I rolled my eyes. "Nothing happened. We talked, we had drinks, he brought me back like a gentleman—no funny business."

Tremaine sighed dramatically. "See, this is why I can't deal with you. If it were me, I'd be testing the limits of that gentleman's behavior."

Dana cackled. "Tremaine, you test limits for sport."

I laughed, shaking my head. "Listen, I like him, but I don't trust myself. And honestly, I don't trust men like I used to."

Dana exhaled. "Girl, I get it. And not to make this about me, but since we're having a true confession moment..."

Tremaine and I turned to her as she set down her glass and rubbed her temples.

"Remember when I told y'all Trey and I were in a rough patch?" she said slowly.

I frowned. "Yeah..."

Dana took a deep breath. "Well, there's more to it. Trey...he told me—through his therapist, mind you—that he had been flirting with one of his new interns."

Tremaine's mouth dropped. "Oh, hell no."

I sat forward. "Wait. What?"

Dana nodded, looking exhausted. "He swore it didn't go beyond that, that it was just his way of feeling some sort of validation because of everything he's going through." She clenched her jaw. "But do you know how humiliating that was for me? To sit there, like a supportive wife, and hear that my husband—the man I've been bending over backward for—was out here getting attention from some young-ass intern?"

Tremaine shook her head. "I will cut him."

I sighed, rubbing Dana's shoulder. "I don't even know what to say."

Dana took a shaky breath. "I haven't told anyone but y'all. I didn't even tell the boys. And part of me wonders if I would've ever found out if he hadn't been in therapy."

Tremaine leaned back, crossing her arms. "So, what are you gonna do?"

Dana scoffed. "Hell if I know! Right now, I just need a break from thinking about it. And honestly, I'm glad I came on this trip with y'all. I needed this."

We sat in silence for a moment before Tremaine raised her glass. "Alright. To the bullshit men put us through—but also, to us. Because no matter what these fools do, we always got each other."

Dana and I clinked our glasses against hers.

"To us," I murmured.

And as much as my heart was still tangled up in uncertainty about Robert, James, and now David, I knew one thing for sure: My girls. They were my safe place.

And in a world full of uncertainties, that meant everything.

Chapter 40

Tremaine: Transformation

"Baby steps, my ass," I muttered, surveying the organized chaos of my living room.

Piles labeled Keep, Donate, and Trash surrounded me, each one a testament to years of accumulated memories—and let's be real, some questionable life choices.

I was finally convinced that decluttering my space equated to decluttering my mind.

After a few therapy sessions, I realized that holding on to physical clutter was like holding on to mental baggage. Studies have shown that decluttering can boost mood and promote relaxation.

I picked up an old photo of Malik and me at some gala. *Why did I even keep this?* Tossing it into the *Trash* pile, I felt a weight lift off my shoulders. Next, a bracelet Max had given me. Cute, but not my style. Into the *Donate* pile it went.

As I cleaned and tossed, my mind drifted on the past few days since returning home from my girls' getaway with Dana and Joanie. I had thought it would be arduous confronting Malik and Max, but once my mind was made up, I was at a point of no return. I knew it had to be done, and so I did it.

I wasn't about to ghost them; that's not my style. I called Malik first. I took a deep breath and dialed his number. He answered on the second ring.

"Hey, Tre. What's up?"

"Malik, I've been doing some thinking," I began, keeping my tone steady. "What we had was fun, but it's not aligning with where I'm headed. I wish you well, but it's time we part ways."

He sighed, a sound more resigned than surprised. "I get it. Take care, Tre."

I didn't even trip when he didn't put up a fight. Whatever, I guess. I supposed that emergency that had him running back to his wife during our last encounter must've put things back on track for them. Whatever.

Ending things with Malik was a necessary step in my journey toward self-discovery and growth. I felt a sense of closure, ready to embrace the new path I was carving for myself.

Next, Max.

I took a deep breath and dialed Max's number. He picked up after a couple of rings.

"Hey, Tremaine! What's going on?"

"Hey, Max. I've been reflecting on things, and I appreciate the times we've shared, but I'm moving in a different direction now. I hope you understand."

There was a brief pause before he responded. "Of course, Tremaine. You gotta do what's best for you. I wish you all the best."

After ending things with Malik and Max, I felt a mix of relief and disbelief. All that sweating for nothing—those men acted like they could care less. Hell, and why did I get the feeling like I might've made things more convenient for them by calling things off. Who knows? At any rate, this went smoother than I thought it would be. But just in case, I blocked both their asses and deleted their contact information. After all, I'm still in therapy, just got back in church, and I didn't trust them or me at this point. Real talk.

With that chapter closed, I felt a newfound sense of freedom and clarity. It was time to focus on me and the path ahead.

Later that evening, my phone buzzed with Joanie's name flashing on the screen.

"Hey, girl! What's up?"

"Hey, Tremaine. Just wanted to check in. How are you feeling after everything?"

"Honestly? Lighter. Like a weight's been lifted. Therapy's been helping me see things clearer, you know?"

"I get that. I've been very busy focusing on our fundraiser event."

"I understand. I've been doing some reflecting myself. Church has been filling some voids I didn't even realize were there. It's stirred up my passion for teaching again. The lead administrator of the church's development and leadership teams has even suggested I give some thought to leading one of the women's growth groups, 'cause you know *Pastor* Kim's ass has been running her big mouth telling folks that I'm a retired college professor."

"Really? That's amazing, Tremaine! And *ummm,* speaking of *Pastor* Kim, you might want to work on your profanity before you start your instructor gig at the church, girlfriend!"

"Yeah, you're right. It's a bit different from my usual curriculum and how I teach—you know I'm known for being raw—but they think my background and ability to relate to women's experiences would be a good fit. I'll adapt, girl. I know how to censor myself." We both chuckled.

"In that case, sounds like a perfect match. It's funny how therapy and faith can open up new paths for us," Joanie said.

"Absolutely. It's all about growth and embracing new opportunities," I replied. "Also, did I tell you? I've started purging around here. I have countless boxes of old stuff I haven't worn in years and other items that I'm donating to the women's shelter. I've also cleaned my house, reorganized some rooms, and you know, I feel pretty damn good about it."

"You did whaaat?!" Joanie screamed on the other end of the phone. "Who are you, and what have you done with my friend Tremaine?"

I laughed. "I know, right? Who would've thought I'd turn into Ms. Clean and Organized? But honestly, it's been therapeutic. Feels like I'm clearing out old energy, making space for new blessings."

"That's incredible, Tremaine. I'm so proud of you. Next thing I know, you'll be leading a decluttering workshop at the church."

"*Ha!* Let's not get carried away. But seriously, it's amazing how much lighter I feel. It's like shedding old skin."

"I can imagine. It's inspiring, really. Maybe I should tackle that storage closet I've been avoiding for years."

"Go for it, girl. Trust me, once you start, you won't want to stop. And the women's shelter will appreciate the donations."

"You're right. It's a win-win. Thanks for the motivation, Tremaine."

"Anytime, Joanie. We're all on this journey together, right?"

"Absolutely. Here's to new beginnings and open spaces."

"Cheers to that!"

As we ended the call, I couldn't help but smile. Sharing my progress with Joanie made it all the more real and rewarding. I was embracing change, and it felt exceptionally great.

Chapter 41

Dana: Unbreakable Bond

Returning home from Houston, I felt a renewed sense of clarity. The trip with Joanie and Tremaine had been a balm to my weary soul, but now it was time to face the reality awaiting me. Trey and I had hit a rough patch—there was no denying that—yet, deep down, I knew our love was strong enough to weather this storm.

I found Trey in the living room, the soft hum of the television filling the space. He looked up as I entered, a mixture of relief and apprehension in his eyes.

"Hey," he greeted softly.

"Hey," I replied. "The boys gone?"

"Yeah. I knew you'd be coming in tonight, so I told them they could go on ahead and leave. How was your trip?"

"It was good. We need to talk."

He nodded, muting the TV. "I know."

I sat down on the sofa next to him. Taking a deep breath, I began, "Trey, I love you, and I know you love me, but this...situation with the intern, it hurt me deeply. Even if it was just for validation, it felt like a betrayal, especially given everything we're going through with your health."

He looked down, guilt evident on his face. "Dana, I'm so sorry. I never meant to hurt you. I was feeling...inadequate, and her attention made me feel seen. But it was a mistake—a stupid, thoughtless mistake."

I nodded, tears welling up. "I understand that you were seeking validation, but it made me question if I'm enough for you. I've been by your side through everything, and it hurts to think that wasn't sufficient."

Trey reached out, taking my hand. "You are more than enough, babe. My actions were about my own insecurities, not a reflection of you or our relationship. I need to work on communicating my feelings better rather than seeking affirmation elsewhere."

I squeezed his hand, appreciating his honesty. "We both have our insecurities. I sometimes fear losing you, especially with your health challenges. Maybe I've been so focused on being strong for you that I haven't shared my own vulnerabilities."

He looked into my eyes, his voice soft. "Let's promise to be more open with each other—to share our fears and doubts, no matter how difficult. I don't want any more secrets between us, and I damn sure don't want to lose you over some bullshit."

I nodded, a sense of relief washing over me. "Agreed. And I don't want to lose you either. No more secrets. We'll face our insecurities together, as a team."

We sat in silence for a moment, the weight of our words settling between us. Finally, I spoke. "I want us to work through this, Trey. I believe what we have is worth fighting for."

He squeezed my hand, tears glistening in his eyes. "It is, babe. It absolutely is."

That night, as we prepared for bed, there was a palpable shift between us. Trey, despite his ongoing treatments, seemed more present than he had in months.

As we lay together, he turned to me, his expression tender. "I miss being close to you."

I smiled softly. "I've missed it too."

We knew that traditional intimacy might be challenging given his condition, but we were determined to find new ways to connect. We explored gentle touches, shared lingering kisses, and whispered words of love and reassurance. It was different from our past encounters, but it was deeply fulfilling—a new kind of passion that honored our current reality.

As we held each other tighter, a sense of peace washed over me. We had faced the darkness together and emerged stronger. Our love had evolved, adapting to the challenges life had thrown our way.

In that moment, I knew that no matter what the future held, we would face it hand in hand, our bond unbreakable.

Chapter 42

Joanie: Swift Transitions

Back at my gallery, the familiar scent of oil paints and aged wood surrounded me, offering a comforting embrace. The weekend in Houston with Dana and Tremaine had been a delightful escape—filled with laughter, deep conversations, and a rekindling of our sisterhood.

But amid all the cherished moments, my thoughts kept drifting back to David. Since returning home, he'd called me twice, each time just to check in and express how wonderful it was to see me again.

Our conversation at the exhibit had been unlike any I'd had with Robert or James. David's genuine interest in my life over the past forty years was both surprising and refreshing.

He leaned in, his eyes reflecting sincere curiosity. "Joanie, what has been the most fulfilling part of your journey in the art world?"

I paused, taken aback by the depth of his question. "Well, mentoring young artists has been incredibly rewarding. Seeing them find their unique voice and flourish...it's indescribable."

He smiled warmly. "That's beautiful, and what inspired you to open your own gallery?"

As I shared my story—the challenges, the triumphs, the moments of doubt—David listened intently, occasionally nodding or asking thoughtful follow-up questions.

"How did you overcome those moments when you felt like giving up?" he inquired, his tone gentle.

"Leaning on friends like Dana and Tremaine and reminding myself why I started in the first place," I replied, feeling a warmth spread through me.

Throughout our conversation, I found myself opening up about personal experiences I'd rarely discussed with anyone, let alone a man. David's presence made me feel seen and heard in a way I hadn't experienced in years.

As I stood in the quiet of my gallery, I couldn't help but smile, reflecting on the unexpected reconnection with an old friend who had effortlessly reignited a spark within me.

My thoughts wandered back, reminiscing about the weekend with Dana and Tremaine and the unexpected reconnection with David, my Apple Watch chimed, pulling me back to the present. It was time for a virtual meeting with my daughters to finalize details for our upcoming fundraiser scholarship event.

I quickly set up my laptop and joined the call. My eldest, Layla, appeared first, her backdrop showcasing the bustling energy of New York City.

"Hi, Mom!" Layla greeted with a bright smile. "I have some exciting news. I've secured Mickalene Thomas as our keynote speaker."

My eyes widened in astonishment. "Mickalene Thomas, the renowned mixed-media artist known for her vibrant, rhinestone-studded portraits celebrating Black women?"

"Yes, that's her," Layla confirmed. "She's thrilled to be part of our event."

"That's incredible, Layla! Her work is so impactful, exploring and expanding traditional notions of female identity and beauty."

As we continued discussing the event, my youngest daughter, Aisha, joined the call from Dallas.

"Hey, everyone," Aisha chimed in. "I have some great news too. I've connected with a few emerging Black artists from the DFW area who are eager to participate."

"That's wonderful, Aisha," I replied. "The African American Museum in Dallas is currently showcasing the 28th Biennial Carroll Harris Simms National Black Art Competition and Exhibition, highlighting the talents of Black artists. Perhaps we can collaborate with some of the featured artists."

"Great idea, Mom," Aisha agreed. "This will add a rich local dimension to our event."

After finalizing the event details with Layla and Aisha, the conversation took an unexpected turn.

"Mom," Layla began, a mischievous glint in her eye, "have you had any interesting developments in your personal life lately?"

I raised an eyebrow. "What do you mean?"

"Oh, you know," Aisha chimed in. "Any new friends? Maybe someone special?"

I felt a blush creep up my cheeks. "Well, I have been seeing someone—dating, to be more exact."

Both of them leaned closer to their screens, eyes wide with excitement.

"Spill the tea, Mom!" Layla urged. "Who is he? What's his name? How did you meet?"

I chuckled at their enthusiasm. "His name is David. We reconnected at an art exhibit in Houston. We knew each other back in college."

"College? That's like, what, forty-sumthin' years ago?" Aisha teased. "Talk about a blast from the past."

"Very funny," I replied, rolling my eyes. "Yes, it's been a long time, but we've been catching up, and it's been...nice."

"Nice?" Layla echoed. "Come on, Mom. We need more than that. Is he coming to the event? Do we get to meet him?"

I shook my head, smiling. "The event is about celebrating art and culture, not my personal life. I doubt he'll be there. Maybe in the future, there will be time for introductions."

Aisha pouted playfully. "Fine, but don't keep us waiting too long. We want to make sure he's good enough for our mom."

I laughed, feeling a warmth in my heart. "I promise, when the time is right, you'll be the first to know."

As we wrapped up the call, I couldn't help but feel grateful for my daughters' support and curiosity. Life had a funny way of bringing unexpected joys, and I was learning to embrace them, one day at a time.

Yet, as I sat back, a pang of guilt tugged at me. I hadn't been entirely truthful with Layla and Aisha. I had kept my relationships with Robert and James from them, not wanting to burden them with the complexities of my personal life. Now, with David reentering my world, I wondered if my secrecy had been a disservice to the open relationship I cherished with my daughters.

Reflecting on how the past and present were intertwining—from reconnecting with David to collaborating with my daughters on this meaningful event—I realized that life, with all its unexpected turns, was proving to be a masterpiece in its own right. Perhaps it was time to embrace honesty, not just with myself, but with those I loved most.

Chapter 43

Joanie: Sweet Comparisons

As I sat in the dimly lit gallery, the soft hum of the city outside, I couldn't help but reflect on the whirlwind of my recent events. It was like my relationships, both past and present, seemed to intertwine in a complex dance, each step revealing more about myself than the partners I'd chosen.

David had brought a refreshing ease into my life—a stark contrast to the meticulously orchestrated dates with James. I realized that while James checked all the boxes on paper, our connection lacked the raw, unfiltered intimacy I craved. Initially James' perfection seemed appealing, then it soon felt suffocating, leaving little room for genuine connection. His need for control over every detail left little room for genuine moments.

Our dates had been nothing short of spectacular. James was the epitome of a gentleman: always punctual, impeccably dressed, and with an itinerary that could rival a royal engagement. Yet, beneath the surface of candlelit dinners and helicopter rides, something was amiss. There was a lack of spontaneity, a missing depth in our conversations. It felt as though we were actors in a well-rehearsed play, each following a script.

It became clear that our relationship, though pleasant, wasn't fulfilling my deeper desires.

In the midst of planning the upcoming event and savoring the effortless moments with David, I'd unintentionally sidelined James. It wasn't out of malice; life had simply flowed in a different direction.

Realizing the need to address this lingering thread, I decided to reach out to James. After all, everyone deserves honesty. I picked up my phone and dialed his number, the ringing echoing my apprehension.

"Joanie, it's good to hear from you, how've you been?" James answered, his voice warm and familiar.

"Hi, James. I've been well. Thank you. Listen, I was hoping you'd have some time today to come by the gallery for a chat."

"Of course. Is everything alright?"

I took a deep breath, gathering my thoughts. "Yes. Everything's fine. What time should I expect you?"

He chuckled softly. "Actually, I'm free in about an hour—just finishing up a class. I'll head over to your spot as soon as I'm done here. Does that work for you?"

I tried to keep my voice light, appreciating his willingness to oblige me. "Perfect. I'll see you then. The gallery will be closed, but I'll be here waiting."

After ending the call, I felt a mix of relief and nervousness. To be on the safe side, I texted Tremaine to let her know about the meeting.

She replied promptly: *Girl, I will call you in an hour to make sure his ass is gone. If he's still there, at least he'll know someone is aware you're not alone, so he'll have to go.*

An hour had passed, I prepared myself, the dim lighting casting long shadows across the artwork. When James arrived, his usual confident demeanor was evident, but there was a hint of curiosity in his eyes.

"Joanie," he greeted, stepping into the gallery's intimate ambience. "This place always feels so serene after hours."

"I'm glad you think so," I replied, offering a small smile. "Thank you for coming on such short notice."

He nodded, his gaze searching mine. "Of course. What's on your mind?"

I gestured toward a nearby seating area, and we both settled into the plush chairs. Taking a moment to gather my thoughts, I began, "James, I've enjoyed the time we've spent together. Your attention to detail, the care you've shown—it's been wonderful."

He smiled, but there was a flicker of apprehension. "But?"

"But," I continued gently, "I've come to realize that while our dates have been delightful, there's a certain...spontaneity and depth that I find myself missing. It's as if everything is perfectly in place, yet something essential is absent."

James looked down, absorbing my words. "I see."

"It's not about you doing anything wrong," I added quickly. "It's more about what I feel I need at this point in my life. And I think it's only fair to be honest with you about that."

He took a deep breath, then met my gaze. "I appreciate your honesty, Joanie. I can't say I'm not disappointed, but I understand."

A moment of silence settled between us, filled with unspoken sentiments.

" I know we've decided to part ways, but I was hoping to attend your upcoming event. I believe in the cause and would like to show my support." James said, breaking the quiet.

His request caught me off guard. I hesitated, unsure of how to respond. "James, I–I don't know if that's a good idea."

"I assure you, my intentions are purely supportive," he interjected. "I don't want to cause any discomfort. If you'd prefer I didn't attend, I'll respect that."

Feeling cornered and not wanting to seem unreasonable, I relented. "Alright. If you truly wish to support the event, you're welcome to attend."

"Thank you, Joanie. I appreciate it."

After he left, I couldn't shake a lingering unease.

Later that evening, I felt the need to discuss this unexpected turn. I initiated a FaceTime call with Dana and Tremaine, my pillars of wisdom.

Dana's face appeared first, her reading glasses perched on her nose. "Hey, Joanie! What's up?"

Tremaine joined shortly after, a silk bonnet adorning her head. "This better be good, pulling me away from my shows."

I chuckled, then recounted my conversation with James.

Dana raised an eyebrow. "So, he still wants to come? Even after you ended things?"

Tremaine didn't mince words. "Girl, that's suspect. He might have a hidden agenda."

I sighed, voicing my concerns. "I thought about that, but he seemed sincere. He said he believes in the cause and wants to support it."

Dana leaned closer to the screen. "Just be cautious. It's a bit unusual for an ex to insist on attending such events."

Tremaine nodded in agreement. "Keep your eyes open, Joanie. Don't let your guard down."

Dana exchanged a glance with Tremaine. "Yeah, I'm with Tre. That sounds...suspect. Sounds like he has another motive, but what could it be?"

Then Dana added thoughtfully, "Or perhaps he wants closure on his terms. Attending the event could be his way of feeling in control or showing that he's still present in your life."

I considered their perspectives, feeling the tension building in my neck and shoulders, tightening from the stress of the conversation. "I hadn't thought of it that way. I just didn't want to be rude by telling him not to come."

Tremaine's voice softened, offering support. "Look, Joanie, it's your event. You have every right to decide who should be there.

If his presence is going to make you uncomfortable or complicate things, it's okay to set boundaries."

Dana concurred. "Absolutely. And if he does show up, we'll be there to support you. We can run interference if needed, keep things light, and ensure he doesn't monopolize your time or cause any drama."

Feeling a wave of gratitude, I smiled. Their words resonated with me. "Thank you, both of you. I feel better knowing I have you in my corner. But to let you ladies know, we always have a team of hired security on hand for these events, so I'm not too worried in that regard. We have to protect our assets and such."

The event was fast approaching; I knew I had to stay vigilant. I needed to ensure that the evening remained focused on the art and the cause, without any distractions on any of my personal entanglements overshadowing it.

Chapter 44

Joanie: A Night to Remember

A s I stood in the venue, adjusting a centerpiece, I couldn't help but reflect on how far I'd come. There was a time when I'd second-guess every decision, always worrying about what others thought. Now, I trust my instincts.

Tremaine paused from arranging place settings and looked up, a proud smile spreading across her face. "Girl, you've transformed this place into a masterpiece. Your vision is evident in every detail."

Reviewing the guest list, Dana nodded in agreement. "Absolutely. It's inspiring to see you lead with such confidence."

As we continued our preparations, Tremaine chuckled, a hint of nostalgia in her eyes. "Remember when I'd deflect everything with a joke? Therapy's taught me it's okay to be real, to let my guard down."

I placed a hand over my heart, feigning shock. "We've noticed. It's refreshing to see this side of you."

Dana turned her head abruptly, her expression earnest. "Your openness has brought us even closer. You've been on quite the journey, Tre."

Finalizing the seating arrangements, Dana walked toward me. "I've decided to decline a consulting offer that would've clashed with this event. And the boys agreed to come to the event to sit with Trey. He's insisted on being here, but I told him I'm on duty tonight, so I'm not going to be at his every beck and call. The doctor said he's doing exceptionally well in his recovery, so no guilt. Besides, Trey knows how important this event is to you, Joanie, and how important it is for us to be here to support you, Layla, and Aisha on such a worthy cause. This is the new me, and it's time I prioritize what's truly important to me and for me."

I looked at my friend in admiration. "That's a big step for you, putting you and your personal commitments first."

Tremaine reached over and lightly touched Dana's hand. "Girl, I'm so proud of you for setting those boundaries, Dana."

As I stood in the venue, the ambience was nothing short of breathtaking. The room was adorned with an exquisite collection of African-American paintings and artifacts, each piece meticulously curated to celebrate our rich heritage. The walls showcased vibrant works from renowned artists, their canvases telling stories of resilience, culture, and history. Strategically placed sculptures and artifacts added depth, offering a tangible connection to our past.

At the heart of the room stood the silent auction table, elegantly draped and illuminated to highlight the centerpiece—a generous donation from our esteemed speaker. The artwork, a mesmerizing blend of colors and textures, drew the eye and promised to be the highlight of the evening. The table also featured an array of other coveted items, each thoughtfully presented to entice potential bidders.

The lighting cast a warm, inviting glow, enhancing the elegance of the setting. Every detail, from the floral arrangements to the seating, was designed to create an atmosphere of sophistication and cultural pride. As I took it all in, I felt a swell of pride and anticipation for the evening ahead.

Taking a step back, I surveyed the room. "Well, ladies, I think we've done all that needs to be done here. The rest will be handled by the waitstaff. Oh, and Layla and Aisha have a team of young ladies as greeters and hostesses. Security is here already too. We can't have these masterpieces here without them!" I chuckled. "We can head out, get showered, have our faces beat, and our outfits on. I can't wait to see how this all comes together."

As we gathered our belongings, the bond between us felt stronger than ever, each of us embracing our growth and our unbreakable bond.

The evening had finally arrived, and the venue was nothing short of enchanting. The room looked even more inviting than it did earlier when we were there. The radiant and strategically placed lighting bathed the artwork in the room. I watched as our guests milled around the room conversing and admiring the exquisite collection of African-American paintings and artifacts, each piece thoughtfully curated and strategically placed to captivate their tastes. Subtle accent lights highlighted intricate details, while soft diffused illumination created an interplay of light and shadow, drawing potential art buyers to the finest elements of rich textures and vibrant colors. The artwork created an atmosphere that was both elegant and welcoming.

As I surveyed the elegantly adorned venue, my eyes were drawn to a familiar figure standing near the silent auction table—a man draped in a black dinner jacket, crisp white shirt, and bow tie. Under the low-key lighting, I thought I was imagining things, but no, it was Jackson. Not wanting to draw attention to his presence, I veered in the opposite direction, deciding to check on David to ensure his seating was satisfactory and to touch base before our keynote speaker took the stage. I was determined not to let anything or anyone disrupt the evening's charitable endeavors.

As I mingled with the guests, I couldn't help but feel a swell of pride seeing my daughters, Layla and Aisha, gracefully engaging with attendees, their poise reflecting the essence of the event. Nearby, Tremaine was in her element, effortlessly balancing humor and charm as she conversed with a group of art enthusiasts.

During the planning stages for the evening, we'd made a collective decision to mix things up—no cliques, no comfort zones. Instead of sitting together like we always did, we agreed to strategically seat ourselves and our guests at different tables throughout the room. The goal was simple: to keep the energy flowing, spark fresh conversations, and ensure no one felt left out or boxed in. It was about presence, poise, and connecting with as many people as possible.

Tremaine had surprised me and Dana. She had taken a leap of faith, in keeping with our plan, she had invited a distinguished gentleman she'd met at church to join our event this evening. His presence added a touch of intrigue, and she'd seated him at her assigned table. When I saw this, I'd kind of wished we had all been at the same table, just so we could've gotten a better read on him during dinner.

Dana arrived with Trey and their sons. Their youthful energy added a lively dynamic to the evening, and I noticed Dana keeping a watchful yet relaxed eye on them, allowing herself to enjoy the night.

As I approached the silent auction table to check on the bids, I spotted Jackson standing there with an air of nonchalance. Our eyes locked, and there was no avoiding the confrontation. I steeled myself, maintaining a composed exterior.

"Jackson," I began, keeping my tone neutral, "what brings you here?"

He offered a casual smile, glancing around the room before settling his gaze back on me. "Good to see you, Joanie. I've reached out, but you haven't responded. I was concerned, so I thought I'd come support your event and see how you're doing."

I felt a mix of emotions bubbling beneath the surface but kept them in check. "As you can see, I'm doing well. Enjoy the evening."

Without waiting for a reply, I turned on my heel and walked away, determined to keep the night's focus on the cause at hand and avoid any unnecessary tension, especially with David present.

Just as I steadied myself, I felt a tap on my shoulder. Turning, I was met with James' warm smile.

"Joanie, this event is spectacular."

"Thank you, James. I'm glad you could make it."

Before he could respond, Malik and Veronica approached. Veronica, an avid art lover, was effusive in her praise.

"Joanie, the curation tonight is simply divine."

"Thank you, Veronica. It means a lot coming from you."

Malik and Veronica moved on. I couldn't shake the feeling that Veronica's presence had another layer, perhaps more personal than just the art.

The night was a delicate dance of navigating past and present relationships. I found solace in brief moments with Tremaine and Dana, their humor and support providing much-needed relief.

At one point, Tremaine sidled up to me, a mischievous glint in her eye.

"Girl, if this gets any more like a soap opera, we're gonna need commercial breaks."

I stifled a laugh, grateful for her levity.

I managed to regain my composure after the episode with Jackson and James; I remained vigilant, ensuring that interactions remained cordial and that the focus stayed on the event's purpose. Despite the underlying tensions, I was on task to make this night a success. And just like the colloquial saying goes—the devil is a lie to think otherwise.

As we settled into our seats, the evening's allure flowed seamlessly, masking the minor hiccups I'd encountered along the way. Only Tremaine and Dana noticed, and we exchanged knowing nods, reaffirming our pact to remain vigilant against any potential distractions. I couldn't help but smirk, imagining us as a trio of covert operatives—Christie Love from *Get Christie Love!*, Robyn McCall from *The Equalizer*, and Simone Clark from *The Rookie: Feds*—guarding our event against any adversaries. In our reality, these adversaries took the form of exes like James, Robert, Max, Jackson, and Malik. Oh, and let's not forget *The Devil Wears Prada* here, live and in living color, Veronica's conniving self. Oh yes, we were more than ready for whatever the night might throw at us.

It felt good to finally be seated. The tables were adorned with crisp linens and flickering candles, casting a warm glow that complemented the rich hues of the artwork surrounding us. The aroma of the forthcoming meal wafted through the air, promising a delightful culinary experience.

David sat beside me, his presence comforting amid the evening's excitement. Layla and Aisha, my beautiful daughters, were engaged in their usual sister-friend girl talk, their eyes sparkling with anticipation and every so often, one of them would give me that look that said, *You have some explaining to do*. It wasn't intentional that they hadn't properly been introduced to David, but things happened so fast and life had been lifing, and before we knew it, here we were. I'd fill them in with the tea later.

Across from us, Tremaine was seated with her mystery date, a distinguished gentleman whose eyes held a hint of intrigue. At a nearby table, Dana, Trey, and their sons were settling in, the young men casting curious glances at the young ladies in attendance.

By the time I was good and settled in my seat, the first course was served—a delicate butternut squash soup garnished with a drizzle of truffle oil and toasted pumpkin seeds—the room hummed with the soft murmur of conversations and the clinking of silverware. Our keynote speaker, Mickalene Thomas, a renowned artist whose work had profoundly impacted the Black art culture, was seated with us, adding an air of distinction to our table. Having Ms. Thomas seated with us was actually one of Layla's ideas. She felt that skipping the traditional dais or speaker's table would create a more relaxed atmosphere—and give everyone a chance to connect with Ms. Thomas on a more personal level. I'll admit, I wasn't completely sold on it at first. But the more I thought about it—especially how much I loathe being the center of attention up on a platform—I came around. And honestly? Layla was right. Watching the evening unfold, I could see how perfectly it worked. The energy was easy, the conversations flowed, and everyone seemed to genuinely enjoy themselves.Between sips of the velvety soup, the conversation naturally flowed toward the significance of the evening. I felt a deep sense of gratitude and inspiration, compelled to share my journey.

"You know," I began, glancing around the table, "art has always been more than just a passion for me. It started as a refuge during challenging times, a way to express emotions I couldn't put into words. Over time, it became a bridge—a means to connect with others and give back to our culture."

Ms. Thomas nodded appreciatively. "Art indeed has a profound impact. It not only fosters self-expression but also aids in building self-esteem and character."

Tremaine's date leaned in, his interest evident. "It's fascinating how creative expression can serve as a therapeutic outlet, promoting mental well-being and community cohesion."

Layla, ever insightful, added, "Engaging in artistic endeavors can be healing. It allows individuals to process experiences and emotions, leading to personal growth."

Aisha chimed in, "And by sharing our art, we contribute to the community's cultural tapestry, inspiring others and fostering a sense of belonging."

The waitstaff discreetly cleared the soup bowls, and the main course arrived—a succulent herb-crusted salmon accompanied by roasted seasonal vegetables and a creamy risotto. The discussion naturally deepened, delving into the transformative power of art.

Dana shared, "I've seen firsthand how art programs can restore individuals to their communities, providing them with purpose and a platform to rebuild their lives."

Ms. Thomas concurred, "Art initiatives have been instrumental in rehabilitation, offering a constructive outlet for expression and skill development."

During the main course, the artist turned to me with a thoughtful expression. "Joanie, I'm curious about the selection process for your scholarship recipients. How do you choose the deserving candidates?"

I smiled, appreciating the opportunity to share our journey. "We host several events throughout the year leading up to this grand evening. Our selection criteria focuses on the applicants' community volunteerism, academic performance, involvement in the arts, and an essay they submit. Tremaine, being a retired university professor, oversees the essay evaluations and has been instrumental in narrowing down the best. So far, we've been fortunate; all our recipients have been exceptional. With the support of our co-sponsors, we haven't had to turn anyone away. Each recipient receives a $2,500 scholarship and a voucher for art supplies to their chosen school or institution. It's been incredibly gratifying."

The artist nodded appreciatively. "That's a comprehensive and impactful approach. It's heartening to see such dedication to nurturing young talent."

As dessert—a decadent chocolate mousse garnished with fresh berries—was served, the conversation took on a more personal tone.

One of Dana and Trey's sons, who had been quietly listening, spoke up. "We've always seen art as something distant, but hearing these stories makes it feel more relatable and impactful."

Their openness sparked a sense of hope within me. "Art has the power to touch lives in unexpected ways. It's a universal language that transcends barriers and unites us."

A jazz ensemble played music in the background as the anticipation grew for the keynote address. When the artist took the stage, the room fell silent. Every guest was captivated by her presence. Her speech was profound. She effortlessly wove personal anecdotes with broader reflections on the transformative power of art. She spoke of art as a universal language, a bridge between cultures, and a catalyst for personal and communal growth.

Following her inspiring words, it was time to present the scholarships. I stood alongside my team, calling each recipient to the stage. The young artists approached, their faces alight with pride and hope. We handed them their awards amid applause, capturing the moments with photographs that would serve as lasting memories of their achievements.

My heart brimmed with emotion. These events always reminded me of my younger self, yearning for a mentor to guide me as we now did for our young recipients. Witnessing the joy on their faces and the unwavering support from their families made every effort worthwhile. The evening ended, and I fondly recalled a mantra my mom used at the close of most every event she would attend—"and now we've come to the end of the rainbow." I smiled.

Several guests approached me, expressing their gratitude and admiration. One attendee remarked, "Thank you for a wonderful event. It's truly inspiring to see such support for the arts and young talent."

Another added, "The atmosphere tonight was electric, and the cause couldn't be more worthy. Congratulations on a successful event."

Their words were touching, reaffirming the importance of our mission and the impact of our collective efforts.

I exhaled a sigh of relief. The last of the guests exited the venue. I felt a profound sense of joy. The event had been a resounding success, and I eagerly yearned for tomorrow's recap with Tremaine and Dana. The new connections forged tonight were invigorating, and while the meal nourished our bodies, the entire experience had rejuvenated our souls. Personally, I felt recharged and inspired. What could possibly go amiss after such an enriching evening? Just as this thought crossed my mind, my phone buzzed with an incoming message. Glancing at the screen, my heart skipped a beat. It was a name I hadn't expected to see.

Chapter 45

Joanie: An Estranged Ghost

*W*hat the...was all I could muster in my thoughts after opening and reading and rereading that text from last night. It was all I could do to keep it together and put up a front in front of Layla, Aisha, Tremaine, Dana, and David.

David. The last person I needed to see me unglued and going through drama, especially past trauma. I shifted in my bed, kicking my leg from beneath the covers. The morning sun seemed much brighter than normal peeking through the curtains as I lay in bed.

The more I tried, the harder it was to ignore the weight of last night's unexpected message pressing heavily on my mind. I don't know the last time I'd heard from my estranged father. His unexpected text had been silenced and confusing.

Why?

After all this time? What did he want? Was he dying? Did he need a kidney? I thought nothing but the worst.

The text read: *Hello, Joanie. It's your dad. I just wanted to reach out to say I'd love to see you. I know it's been a while. This is my number. Save it in your phone. If you feel the same, text me your availability, and we'll go from there. Sorry it's been so long. Love, your dad. Oh, and by the way, congratulations on your success. I've been watching you from afar, and I'm very proud of you and all your accomplishments.*

Really? Just like that? What the hell was he thinking? And what the hell was I supposed to do?

I had always believed I'd forgiven him, attributing our distance to his inability to nurture or parent effectively. But now, with his sudden intrusion into my life, old wounds resurfaced, and I found myself questioning whether I'd truly moved on.

"I swear, I don't have time to deal with this shit right now," I said aloud and got up to use the bathroom.

Hours passed in my contemplative state until the scheduled FaceTime call with Tremaine and Dana. As their faces appeared on the screen, I forced a smile, pushing aside my personal turmoil to focus on our recap of the event.

"Can you believe Malik brought Veronica?" Tremaine began, rolling her eyes.

Dana nodded. "And Jackson showing up unannounced? That was a surprise."

I chuckled, though my thoughts were elsewhere. "Yes. It was quite the evening."

"I'm surprised Robert didn't show up," Dana continued. "He was the only one missing. Oh, and where was Max? Isn't he one of your clients, Joanie?"

Grateful for the distraction, I replied, "He made a sizable contribution last week and mentioned he'd be out of town, so I knew he wouldn't be there."

"Yeah, he probably didn't want to run into Tremaine," Dana teased.

Tremaine shrugged. "Whatever. He's a grown man; he can do as he pleases."

"Am I tripping, or Joanie, you really seem preoccupied. What's on your mind, girlfriend?" Dana asked.

"Girl, I thought it was just me," Tremaine said.

I knew Tremaine and Dana knew me better than anyone had known me in my life, and when I'm bothered, no matter how hard I tried to camouflage it, they know. I let my guard down and gave them the 4-1-1 on my text from my father. After the *ooob*s and *awww*s then much encouragement from Tremaine and Dana, I was persuaded. After much trepidation, I decided to be the grown-ass woman I professed I was and meet with him.

I'd put it off for as long as I reasonably could. Our girl chat had ended hours ago. I typed in the text box, backspaced, retyped, and typed again, finally settling on a text to my estranged father.

Tomorrow, 5PM Biscuit Bar—Dallas. Google it.

In my mind, this was a neutral ground where we could talk without distraction.

Within moments, he texted back, *I'll see you there. Looking forward to it.*

As I entered the venue, I spotted him at a corner table, nervously stirring his coffee. He looked older than I remembered—the years etched deeply into his face. Taking a deep breath, I approached and sat across from him.

"Joanie," he began, his voice trembling slightly, "thank you for agreeing to meet."

I nodded, unsure of what to say. "It's been a long time."

He sighed, looking down at his cup. "Too long. I know I haven't been the father you deserve. Leaving you and your mother...it was the biggest mistake of my life."

I felt a surge of emotion but kept my peace. "Why now? After all these years, why reach out?"

He looked up, his eyes glistening. "I've been following your accomplishments, seeing the incredible woman you've become. It made me realize how much I've missed and how much I've lost. I want to make amends, if you'll let me."

I studied him, searching for sincerity. "You hurt me deeply. Your absence...it left scars. I've had to learn to trust again, to open up to people."

He nodded, tears slipping down his cheeks. "I can't change the past, but I'm here now, willing to do whatever it takes to earn your forgiveness."

I looked at him, seeing a reflection of my own struggles in the dating world—the fear of vulnerability, the hesitation to trust.

His attempt to reconnect mirrored my own journey of being vulnerable to new relationships.

"Forgiveness isn't easy," I said softly, "but maybe we can start with getting to know each other again."

A hopeful smile spread across his face. "I'd like that very much."

As we sat there, delving into our pasts and sharing our present lives, my father suddenly leaned forward, his eyes earnest. "Joanie, don't play yourself short. You're brilliant. The way you've built your life, your career, it's nothing short of inspiring."

His words caught me off guard, stirring emotions I hadn't anticipated. In that moment, I realized that opening my heart to him was not just about mending our fractured relationship but also about healing parts of myself I had long ignored. Facing the past with him allowed me to find a new strength to embrace the future, both in love and in life.

As the conversation flowed, I found solace in the familiar banter, temporarily setting aside the emotional upheaval caused by my father's message. Yet, deep down, I knew I couldn't avoid confronting these resurfaced feelings forever. And right now, in this moment, I was glad I'd been the grown-ass woman I'd always professed to be and faced one of the things from my past that I believed no longer held me bondage.

Epilogue

Joanie: Lifing Full Circle

As I sat on my bed preparing for my morning workout, the events of the past few months flooded my mind. Sunlight streamed through the open blinds—a daily ritual I cherished, embracing the mantra: "Let there be light."

Life had unfolded in unexpected ways, particularly with the cautious steps my father and I had taken toward reconciliation. Before our initial meeting, I had rehearsed countless conversations in my mind, bracing for unresolved grievances. Yet, when I saw the fragility etched on his face, the weight of time having already exacted its toll, any desire for retribution melted away.

Our eyes met, and I sensed his sincerity. He began to speak, his voice tinged with regret.

"Joanie," he began, his gaze steady yet remorseful, "I've carried the burden of my absence every day. Leaving you was the greatest mistake of my life."

I swallowed hard, emotions swirling. "Why now, Dad, after all these years?"

He sighed, looking down at his hands. "Fear. Pride. I was a coward, unable to face the pain I caused. But I've been following your life from afar, and I'm so proud of the woman you've become. I hoped maybe it's not too late to make amends."

Tears welled up as I listened to him recount stories from my childhood, moments I thought he'd forgotten. He spoke of his failures, his lack of courage, and finally, with a trembling voice, he said, "I'm sorry, Joanie. I don't deserve it, but I hope you can find it in your heart to forgive me."

A heavy silence enveloped us. I took a deep breath, feeling the weight of years lift slightly. "I forgive you, Dad. Let's not dwell on the past. We have the present to make things right."

From that moment, our relationship transformed. He became protective, introducing me proudly as his baby girl to everyone we met. We established a ritual of meeting regularly, sharing stories, and bridging the chasm of lost years. Each conversation, though tentative, brought healing and understanding, mending the fractures of our past.

David became an integral part of my world and introducing him to Layla and Aisha was a significant milestone. I remember the evening vividly: We decided on a casual dinner at my home to keep things comfortable.

As the girls arrived, I could sense their curiosity. David, with his warm smile, greeted them at the door.

"Hi, Layla and Aisha. I've heard so much about you both," he said, extending a hand.

Layla shook his hand first, her eyes assessing. "Nice to finally get a chance to formally meet you, David. Mom's told us a bit about you too."

Aisha nodded, adding, "Yeah, there was so much happening the night of the event that we never really got properly introduced. So Mom says you're into art as much as she is."

David chuckled. "Guilty as charged. I even brought over a piece from my collection to show you all."

Throughout dinner, the conversation flowed easily. David shared stories from his travels, and the girls opened up about their recent projects and interests. The atmosphere was light, filled with laughter and genuine connection.

As the evening progressed, Layla leaned over to me and whispered, "Mom, he's pretty cool."

Aisha nodded in agreement. "Yeah. I like him."

My heart swelled with relief and joy. Seeing my daughters accept David so warmly was more than I had hoped for.

Our families began to intertwine seamlessly. David's four adult children—Michael, Hope, Murray, and Emily—were equally welcoming. We organized a weekend getaway to Gulf Shores in Alabama for relaxation and some outdoor activities, giving everyone a chance to bond.

One evening, as we sat at a lively beachfront restaurant with a live quartet, Michael spoke up. "You know, it's been a while since we've seen Dad this happy."

Hope nodded. "Agreed. Joanie, you've brought a new light into his life."

I smiled, feeling a warmth that had nothing to do with the music that enveloped us. "And he's brought so much joy into mine."

While wedding bells weren't on the horizon, the harmony we shared painted a picture of a promising future. David and I were on the same page—we didn't feel the need to rush or prove anything to anyone. What we had was solid. If marriage came, it would be because we both truly wanted it, not because of pressure or expectation. For now, we were just good—grown, grounded, and grateful. Our gatherings were lively affairs, filled with laughter, shared stories, and the promise of new memories. The blending of our families wasn't without its challenges, but the love and respect we had for one another made every step of the journey worthwhile.

Tremaine, having faced her past fears about commitment embodied by men like Malik and Max, found solace and purpose within her church's growth group. Drawing from her experiences, she became a beacon of wisdom, guiding others on their journeys. Her newfound confidence was undeniable, and her relationship with her new beau—no longer the mystery man from our event, but Xavier, whom we'd all come to know and genuinely like—was blossoming. What they shared was grounded in mutual respect, grown-folk values, and a refreshing sense of ease.

One afternoon, as we sipped tea under the pergola on my back patio, the air filled with the mingling scents of lilacs, rosemary, and jasmine from the surrounding garden, I couldn't help but express my amazement.

"Girl, I still can't believe you went cold turkey from Max after y'all had been undercover for so long," I said, shaking my head.

Tremaine chuckled, her eyes reflecting a mix of amusement and resolve. "Well, when a man tells you to do what's best for you, that phrase right there lets me know all I need to about what he really thought about me in the first place."

I nodded, feeling a surge of pride for my friend. "You're absolutely right, friend. It's like he didn't want to be the bad guy. Most of them don't. Instead, they drop subtle hints for you to make the final call."

"Damn skippy," Tremaine agreed, her voice firm. "Fool me once, shame on you; fool me twice, shame on me. It's best to leave and heal. I knew it was best, and I haven't looked back."

I reached over, squeezing her hand. "No, you haven't. And if you do, it should only be as a reminder why you left that relationship in the first place."

With her signature feistiness, Tremaine threw her head back and laughed. "*Okayyy. Baaabyyy*, what you said."

Our laughter echoed throughout the backyard, a testament to the strength and resilience we've cultivated over the years. Tremaine's journey from uncertainty to unwavering confidence served as a powerful reminder that embracing one's worth is the first step toward genuine happiness.

Dana and Trey, after weathering their own storms, recommitted to their marriage with renewed vigor. Through therapy and unwavering transparency, they rediscovered the depths of their bond, serving as a testament to enduring love.

One sunny afternoon, Dana and I visited at my gallery, the invigorating and cool scent of eucalyptus permeating through the air. As we sipped our iced tea, I couldn't help but notice the serene glow on her face.

"You look more at peace than I've seen you in a long time, Dana," I remarked, setting my glass down.

Dana smiled, a mixture of relief and gratitude in her eyes. "It's been a journey, Joanie. After Trey's diagnosis, everything seemed to crumble."

"I remember," I said softly. "It was a tough time for both of you."

She nodded. "But in the midst of it, I realized I had to take care of myself to be there for him. I'm so glad I continued my therapy. I never would've been able to focus on my well-being, and I encouraged Trey to do the same."

"How's he doing now?" I asked.

A warm glow spread across Dana's face as she began to speak. "His prognosis is much better. He's regained his strength, and the color has returned to his skin. More than that, he's become more attentive, more present."

"That's wonderful to hear," I said, reaching out to squeeze her hand, "but how are you holding up?"

Dana took a deep breath. "Honestly, learning to trust him again was challenging. We had to rebuild our foundation. But neither of us wanted to walk away. We love each other too much to give up."

"It sounds like you've both put in the work," I observed.

"We have," she agreed. "And having you and Tremaine by my side has been invaluable. Every woman needs real girlfriends—a sisterhood. Trey is my soulmate, but I also need my own identity, my own space."

"Absolutely," I said, nodding. "We can't pour from an empty cup."

Dana chuckled. "Exactly. Balancing time together—with our sons and for ourselves—has been key. I've learned that taking care of me isn't selfish; it's necessary."

"I'm proud of you," I told her. "You've come a long way."

"Thank you, Joanie," she said, her eyes glistening. "I couldn't have done it without my girls."

As we sat there, the bond of our friendship felt stronger than ever, a testament to the power of support, resilience, and unwavering love.

One evening, as I was wrapping a canvas for a client at my gallery, I reminisced about a recent FaceTime chat with Layla and Aisha. With a blend of humor and humility, I shared some of my past dating escapades.

"Mom," Layla exclaimed, her eyes wide with amusement, "I had no idea you went through all that before meeting David. You've been holding out on us."

Aisha laughed, adding, "Seriously, Mom, you always keep your business so close to your chest."

I chuckled, appreciating their playful curiosity. "Well, some stories are best shared when the time is right. I wanted to set a good example for you both, showing that it's okay to seek out compatible relationships and to value yourself in the process."

Layla nodded thoughtfully. "I get that. It's important to know our worth and not settle."

"Exactly," I replied. "And remember, while having a partner can add richness to your life, true fulfillment comes from within. Live purposefully and with intention."

Aisha smiled warmly. "Thanks, Mom. It's reassuring to know you're always here for us, cheering us on."

"Always," I affirmed. "I'm your biggest advocate, but I'll never intrude. Your lives are your own, and I'm here to support you every step of the way."

As we ended the call, I felt a deep sense of gratitude for the open and respectful relationship I shared with my daughters. Their happiness and growth were my greatest joys, and I was proud to witness the strong, independent women they had become.

I surveyed the tapestry of my life—repaired relationships, deepened friendships, and a love that complemented rather than completed me—I felt a profound sense of gratitude. The most valuable lesson I'd learned was that, as a grown-ass woman, I didn't play when it came to me. The past had shaped me, but it didn't define me. The future was an open canvas, and I was ready to paint it with all the colors of my experiences.

Discussion Questions

1. How do Joanie, Tremaine, and Dana evolve throughout the story? What pivotal moments contribute to their personal growth?

2. In what ways does the story address the challenges and rewards of dating in one's sixties and seventies? How are societal perceptions of older women in romantic relationships portrayed?

3. How do the friendships between the main characters influence their decisions and perspectives? Can you identify instances where their support systems play a crucial role?

4. Discuss Joanie's relationship with her daughters, Layla and Aisha. How does her openness about her dating experiences impact their bond?

5. Joanie's estranged father reaches out after many years. How does this subplot enhance the main narrative? What does it reveal about forgiveness and personal closure?

6. In what ways do the characters find purpose and fulfillment outside of romantic relationships? How is the theme of living intentionally explored?

7. How do the characters confront or conform to societal expectations of women in their age group? Are there moments where they challenge stereotypes?

8. Identify instances where humor is used to cope with adversity. How does this approach affect your perception of the characters and their journeys?

9. How do past relationships influence the characters' present actions and attitudes toward love and companionship?

10. Tremaine's involvement in a church growth group and personal development is highlighted. How does this commitment affect her interactions and self-perception?

11. Joanie's involvement in the arts is a significant aspect of her life. How does this passion influence her relationships and sense of identity?

12. The story concludes without definitive resolutions for all

the characters. How do you feel about this ending? What do you envision for the characters' futures?

About the author

Eartha Gatlin delivers yet another compelling work of literary fiction with *Grown Ass Woman*.

Born and raised in Rockford Illinois, Eartha Gatlin is the talented author behind three captivating books, *The Chronicles of Bria Twon* and *Hey You, What About Me Bria Twon?* and *Who Told You Family is Perfect, Bria Twon?* the third installment in the Bria Twon series. Eartha continues the exploration of women's relatable fiction. As a leader and mentor, Eartha makes it her purpose to tell the stories not shared, with the intention of inspiring women to embrace their best selves. Through her writing, she humorously engages readers, inviting them to see aspects of themselves through the lens of her compelling characters. Beyond her role as an author, Eartha is the proud owner of Ahtrae Publishing, LLC where she has successfully self-published six books, including notable works like *Conflict of Interest* and *No Hope* by author Tyress Cunningham. Currently residing in the dynamic DFW Metroplex, Eartha Gatlin continues to contribute her unique voice and perspective to the literary world.

Stay connected with Eartha Gatlin on Instagram, Facebook, Twitter, LinkedIn, TikTok, and Threads at Author_Eartha Gatlin.

www.ingramcontent.com/pod-product-compliance
Lightning Source LLC
Chambersburg PA
CBHW030125010826
48973CB00002B/422